CRIMSON

Tamela Miles

CRIMSON
Copyright © 2018 by Tamela Miles

ISBN: 978-1-68046-671-3

Published by Satin Romance
An Imprint of Melange Books, LLC
White Bear Lake, MN 55110
www.satinromance.com

Published in the United States of America.

Cover Design by Caroline Andrus

Thank you to my Mom and Dad for encouraging me to push myself that much harder. Thank you to my siblings for bringing joy into my life with your crazy antics. Thank you to my friends for giving me so much support and being that call at 2am. Thanks to the Nightbeasts for the good laughs and caring support in the midnight hour, when all kinds of nocturnal creatures go bump.

ONE

"OH, HURRY THE HELL UP," DELILAH MUTTERED UNDER HER breath, kneading the small black knit bag with nervous hands. She glanced around the place, taking in the dim lighting and scuffed hardwood floors of a bar named Vivian's in a not-so-great area of Downtown Los Angeles. The dark alley she had passed on the way in reeked of hard liquor and rotten food. She had noted, with pity, the few homeless souls taking refuge next to a large dumpster.

She had been waiting here for what seemed like hours for an acquaintance of her younger brother. She was here to handle another one of Declan's situations because he couldn't handle money responsibly. No, she corrected herself. She was here because she felt slightly guilty saying no to Declan whenever he made too many bad bets, which was often. She recognized that he had a gambling problem. It was definitely time to stop babying him before they both ended up like the homeless people outside. Maybe she should even seek professional counseling for him. Her help didn't seem to be enough.

Her eyes darted around the place, pointedly avoiding the lecherous smiles she was getting from a few of the male patrons.

No way in hell did she want to be here too late into the evening, she thought, as the bar's main door opened, letting in a rowdy bunch of people. She could see it was well beyond dusk through the door.

Her gaze settled on one of the men who stepped away from the crowd and looked around the place slowly. He was tall and powerfully built in jeans and leather jacket with the interior lights glinted off his close cropped blond hair. He had already captured most of the female attention in the bar as their heads turned. Not wanting to be caught staring, she glanced away. *The mysterious Ash Lockler, maybe?*

———

Ash had entered the bar in an unobtrusive effort, right behind the raucous crowd of people. His way was to enter a scene quietly, keeping to the shadows of a room. He had to make this quick. This was a simple business transaction and as long as the woman also saw it as such, the smoother things would be.

He saw her right away, the sister. The resemblance between Declan McDade and his sister, the lovely Delilah, was marked. They shared the same dark, curly hair and olive skin. She twisted the long brown strands around two fingers and looked around anxiously.

His smile was small and grim. Declan had become an annoyance and Ash had little patience with him. He wouldn't keep her waiting and approached her table slowly.

"Ash Lockler?" she said, looking up at him. She looked away from his intense gaze for a moment. Clearing her throat, she met his eyes again.

Ash nodded and neatly folded his big frame into the booth, opposite her. He maintained his poker face as he rested his forearms on the table, hands folded. He held her gaze for a moment before he spoke quietly. "I trust you will provide what I expect." He surveyed her pretty face framed by all that long, wildly curly, dark hair. She would do nicely.

Her lips parted to speak, but she hesitated for a moment before nodding slowly. He found her actions amusing, assuming this was her first time in dealing with someone like him. The underworld of vampires and other nocturnal beings was definitely not for this little, gentle mouse. She was beautiful but too timid and nervous for his taste. He caught her staring before she lowered her gaze and reached for her small knit bag.

"Yes. I have it right here. Five thousand cash. You can count it. That should settle my brother's debt to you."

Ash's eyes narrowed in irritation. Declan McDade. The little weasel. Unfortunately for his family, he had grown up to be exactly like his father, Martin. They both shared an unhealthy fascination with underworld dealings. His next words were measured. "I'm afraid that five thousand doesn't even come close to what your brother owes me. His debt is a lot closer to one hundred thousand."

Her lips went slack, and she promptly snapped her mouth shut.

Ash went on. "Your money, in short, is no good. A different sort of payment was arranged between myself and Declan."

"What do you want, then? My house?" Delilah's voice was strangely hoarse, and she took a hasty sip of water.

"No, your house is safe. I want your body on a long- term basis. Anywhere from six months to one year would work," Ash replied simply. She was a blood donor to settle a debt and nothing more, he reminded himself.

The water flew out of her mouth before she could stop it. She wiped her mouth with her fingers. "I'm sorry. Did you just say you want my body?"

Ash nodded, his focus on her full, ripe lips for a few seconds, while he watched a myriad of emotions play across her face. He sensed her shock and anger as her eyes narrowed.

She murmured softly, as if to herself. "This is it – the horrible moment I've always feared. Declan's gambling and whoring has come back to bite us in the ass." Aloud, her tone frosty and expression stony, she told him, "It's not that kind of party, Mr. Lockler." She grabbed her little black bag and left the booth, heading for the main door of the bar.

Ash sighed, rubbing the bridge of his nose in aggravation. Declan McDade had caused him too much inconvenience for quite some time, which was not only sad but dangerous. The kid should be focused on making something good of himself, not living on exorbitant amounts of borrowed cash to fund his debauchery. Maybe it was time for him to just be dead and Ash wouldn't have to deal with this shit anymore. You didn't live as long as he had without knowing a little something about how human emotions work. Surprisingly, the remaining water in her glass hadn't splashed in his face.

He watched Delilah's hips sway in her grey sweater dress and black heels as she exited the bar and he moved quickly to catch her. A woman walking alone at night in this rundown area was begging for trouble.

Delilah was halfway across the crowded parking lot before he gripped her arm. She whipped around, and he instantly felt like one of those pushy people who couldn't let things go and take a simple no for an answer. "Let me go!"

"Declan will pay that debt, one way or the other," Ash said coldly. "I think you would both rather not find out how severe the consequences can be if not."

"Are you threatening us? I offered you five thousand dollars, but my body is not for settling debts. Take what I have and leave us alone."

Ash didn't relish the thought of glamouring her, but he was starving. Untainted human blood was very hard to come by and it was superior in every way to animal blood. He caught her arms and pulled her roughly to him. He smiled and caught her big brown eyes with his. "I'm not going to hurt you and you have no reason to fear me. You and Declan have both known me for years, though you rarely see me." He paused, gauging her facial expressions to see if she was under the spell of his calm, softly spoken words. Now that he had seen her snippy side, some perverse side of him wanted to see how far he could take this with his lies. He was mildly fascinated by her for the moment.

"There's always been an unspoken attraction between you and me, Delilah. We've never explored it, which is probably wise, considering that, if you would let me, I would have you in your home, in the backseat of your car, or up against the wall in the alley. We can argue here in a cold parking lot or we can talk this through at your place. Your choice." He had no intention of trying to screw her, of course. He had plenty of willing female vampires for that. This was all about the blood lust.

He could see she was drowning in his focused gaze. Her knees wobbled, and he held her up. He knew her whole being was focused on his eyes and the cadence of his words. She nodded in acquiescence. "We can go to my home." She paused, looking dazed as she licked her lips. He followed the unconsciously seductive movement with his eyes. "Ash, I feel like…I haven't seen you in a long time," she said.

Ash gave her a reassuring smile. "Yes, Delilah, it's been a long time since we've seen each other. It's the nature of the business I handle, and I wouldn't be here now if it wasn't for Declan's trouble. We'll talk later at your place. You look a little sick. Give me your keys and I'll drive."

———

They were in her house, a modest beige townhouse in Pasadena not far from the Rose Bowl. On arriving, she had invited him in without giving it a second thought. Of course, she was still under the mistaken belief they were old friends. On the drive over, he had concocted an entire history of their friendship, including a friendship with her brother.

"So many vampire books," Ash murmured as he scanned Delilah's crammed bookshelves. There was a small collection of romance novels and thrillers, but there were far more books about vampires.

Delilah smiled and moved to stand next to Ash as she sipped from her glass of red wine. "Vampires are a passion of mine. I thought you knew that about me." Her tone was questioning.

"I was just remarking that there seem to be even more vampire books than the last time I was here," Ash replied smoothly. He picked a book from one of the shelves and read the title aloud. "Blood Lust of the Damned." He snorted. "How appropriate."

His thirst for her blood wasn't easily controlled but he was managing it for the moment. The sweet smell of it pulsing through her veins reminded him why he was willing to settle the exorbitant debt in exchange for her donations. His gaze settled on Delilah's face and he found himself deeply curious about her.

From the dreamy look on her face, he knew she was swimming in a fathomless depth like every human who had been glamoured. He still recalled the dazed feeling of the hypnotic pull before he had been turned. It made one's thoughts disjointed and prevented focusing on one particular notion for very long. It also lowered inhibitions. As he continued to examine her books, his mind conjured up images of his pale skin next to her darker skin as he kissed her. He pushed down his urges.

"Would you like a glass of wine?" She moved away from him and he suspected she was trying to get out of his disturbing orbit, so she could think clearly. He knew her concentration was shot.

"No, thank you," Ash responded, his tone distracted. He shifted his gaze from the books to watch her closely as she sat down on the sofa.

"Have a seat, Ash. Your flight to Denver doesn't leave for a few hours." He sat on a red chair directly across from her and Delilah smiled warmly. "Are you pale all over?"

His eyes were drawn to the contrast of her dark hair and dress against the deep rich red of her sofa. Delilah McDade was an enchanting little thing and snippy as hell when she wasn't glamoured. Her home was also a pleasant surprise, done in crimson and black rather than boring shades of brown and taupe. The colors spoke to him since his own expensive loft in Downtown Los Angeles was decorated completely in black.

"I don't like the sun much."

"Are those beautiful green eyes really contact lenses?"

"All me."

"Why are you so cold? I mean, your skin is practically sub-zero."

"Low blood pressure."

"Will you kiss me?"

Ash hesitated before answering. "As much as I'd really like to, I'm going to say no. Your brother wouldn't appreciate one of his oldest friends hitting on his sister."

Delilah moved without a word and stood directly in front of him. "I'm going to sit in your lap, Ash, and you're going to tell me exactly why we shouldn't be more than friends." She straddled his legs and wrapped her arms around his shoulders. "I've known you forever. Isn't this the next logical step?"

Ash's eyes narrowed thoughtfully. This was a perfect position to simply take what he needed. Very soon, he would be caught up in bloodlust as he'd nearly been back in the parking lot earlier. He smiled at Delilah disarmingly, first stroking her dark hair and then trailing his fingers down her neck. He genuinely liked her. Remarkably, even though he had only known for a couple of hours, she was becoming more than just a blood bag to him. He would take what he needed for the moment and not a drop more. He kissed her neck, and she moaned softly in his ear.

She seemed to thoroughly enjoy his soft, cool lips leaving a trail of goosebumps along her neck. She shivered against him as his tongue traced the shell of her ear. He was about to devour her gorgeous lips when she suddenly pulled away from him. She slapped him. Hard. His fangs shot out immediately and he growled menacingly low in this throat. He grabbed her shoulders.

Delilah gasped in wonder, reaching up to stroke one of his fangs gently. "Vampire," she said in breathless delight. "I was dead on right about you. You are real. My Grammy was from New Orleans, and she told me and my brother all the myths of Southern vampire kingdoms."

Ash shook his head. "The Southern vampire kingdoms are far from a myth. They have existed in secret for centuries and even though every state in the U.S. is now under the rule of one powerful vampire, it wasn't always that way. Your grandmother probably had underground connections to know what she did."

Delilah smiled in remembrance. "Knowing Grammy, I'm certain she did. She insisted she had even met a few in her youth that had her all hot and bothered but we thought she was just telling us a good story." She shook her head slowly. "I'm still not sure if vamps are part of religious folklore or victims of a rare blood disease."

Ash swore under his breath. "A lot of both, but I've never had a crucifix burn me, though I doubt if any of us are God's favorite creatures. Did your grandmother also warn you about the true nature of every vampire? Blood lust rules us at times and it's serious business." His voice was chiding. "Delilah, this is nothing new. You've always known we're real."

She frowned in confusion. He knew she was trying to sort it all out. He was a true life vampire and everything she had dreamed about them was now a part of her reality. "I guess I've always known deep down. My mind is a little cottony right now on some of the details of our friendship, but does Declan know?"

"Yes, of course he knows. Your brother has been involved in some underworld dealings for quite some time. I don't want you to have the mistaken impression that I took advantage by bringing his debt into a situation without him having full disclosure."

She sighed. "No, Declan can easily find trouble on his own. Are there many more of you? Tell me everything." Delilah wrapped her arms around him tightly, resting her face in the crook of his neck and the radiating warmth of her thighs stiffened his cock. He was fighting a losing battle, even though she was only supposed to feed him. Getting sexual with her was definitely a bad idea.

He kept his voice gentle. "You already know everything about me. You just have to remember."

"Well, you'll have to tell me again," she demanded playfully.

Ash's voice was soft and thoughtful as he told her stories of his past. She hung on every word and he caught glimpses of the child she had been. He knew she was in her early thirties with Declan about ten years behind her. He could easily picture what she would look like as an old woman. And, where would he be? Somewhere still under the thumb of the Vampire Council and still trying to come to grips with what he was.

"Tell me more about your past before you became a bad-ass vamp," Delilah said eagerly, still straddling him.

Ash's lip tilted up slightly at the pet name she had adopted for his kind. "I was born Asher John Lockler in 1918. The small town I lived in—Caddo, far up in Northern California—has prospered and is still around today, but I won't dare go back to try to find any of my living family in the foreseeable future. I can't risk being recognized. I am an only child, a miracle child born late in life to my parents, who are buried there. I was turned by my maker when I was 20." He sighed. "Enough talk." He pulled her close and nuzzled her neck.

"Oh, if you need to feed..." Delilah tilted her head back, exposing her throat.

"You would willingly let me feed from you?"

"Of course. What's a little blood between friends?" she quipped.

He laughed at that. Curiosity struck him again, and he pulled back a little. "What do you do for a living now, Delilah?" He watched the fleeting trace of disappointment on her face and laughed inwardly. So eager to be so close to death. He didn't lie to himself. He knew what he was. A little more information about her was all he wanted. His thirst was nearly raging, but he found he needed to satisfy his intense desire to know more about her before taking her blood.

"I'm still a toy design consultant for Kinder Fun," Delilah said. At his blank look, she explained more in detail. "Know that child's game, Bouncin' Blocks? All my work. I created that." She sounded proud of her accomplishment.

Ash nodded in understanding. "Sounds like you're doing well for yourself." He looked around her place again, cataloging every book, rug, and throw pillow.

"After six years at the university earning both of my degrees, I expect nothing less," she replied. She placed her head on his shoulder.

He stroked her hair and she sighed in contentment.

"I take it that a husband and the birth of children will be next for you?" he asked softly, trailing his fingers down her spine. She shivered a bit at his touch.

"Soon, but not now. There's quite a lot I want to do with my life. Then there's Declan to take care of."

The thought of Declan taking advantage of her, even in small ways, pissed him off a little. He had quickly offered up his sister as a blood donor and sex partner to settle a huge debt and had probably expected Delilah to comply. He was nothing more than a low lying snake in high grass, as far as Ash was concerned. He would glamour him later. "Parenthood is a joy that I will probably never experience. I envy you."

"Vamps can't make babies?" Delilah asked slowly.

He shrugged. "I've never tried but it has happened. I suppose if my body temperature was ever warm enough my seed could produce a child. Highly improbable, though."

He kissed the palm of her hand, eyes closed. She planted little kisses on his neck. Ash withstood the sweet torment before his control broke and he kissed her roughly. The moment his tongue met hers, he was overwhelmed by the need to touch her everywhere, to take her. He knew her thoughts were still in a jumble, but he was sure she wanted him just as badly.

Ash quickly unbuttoned the top of her sweater dress, impatiently pushing it down around her waist. Her bra was black lace and he took a moment to appreciate it before unclasping the front, baring her breasts. Shame he would never see the panties. "This will hurt," he said softly as he sank his fangs into the side of one lovely breast. She gasped in shock.

Ash sank into the sweetest maelstrom ever. Her blood was like fragrant honey and drawing blood from her had his skin burning all over, while his cock stiffened against her. She ground her hips and he knew the slight sting of his fangs buried in her skin created a tingling in her core by the faint scent of her arousal. She cupped his head in her hands and murmured encouraging words. He continued until she told him she was dizzy. He retracted his fangs and pulled back to look at her, his lips stained with her blood.

"That was unforgettable. I think that was an orgasm," Delilah said, licking her parched lips. She struggled to stay awake, but her eyelids kept closing. She rested her head on his shoulder as he closed her bra and dress, placing her on the sofa. He watched her drifting off and leaned down to speak softly in her ear.

"Don't worry about your brother's debt. I'll handle everything as an old friend. Consider it paid in full."

He leaned over and kissed her forehead. He didn't dare linger. His thirst had been quenched and she had aroused another great need. He would quickly find another willing human blood donor and sex partner, though finding one to suit his long-term arrangement would be a bit more difficult. Delilah deserved far better than the arrangement he had proposed. She worked hard to support herself and her brother and there was no way in hell she could afford to give him nearly one hundred thousand dollars. He now considered the debt paid in full.

He thought about glamouring her again, to completely erase all of her memories of him and this night. He decided to leave things as they were. He wanted her to remember the one, hot night with a vampire he had given her until she was old woman, telling old stories about his kind, like her Southern grandmother.

Ash left her sleeping and opened her front door. Back to his real life as an undead, such as it was. He was still very much owned by the Vampire Council and his queen. One didn't ignore a summons from them, leaving no place in his life for tender things.

TWO

HER BACK HURT AND HER MOUTH WAS DRY. THOSE WERE THE FIRST things that occurred to Delilah when she awoke the next morning on her sofa, still wearing her dress from the night before. She rose to a sitting position and rubbed her eyes. Sunlight streamed through the big window in her living room and the leaves on the big tree outside rustled in the wind. She smiled, still half asleep, happy for the cold but pleasant winter weather.

Delilah's smile lasted for a brief second before last night's memories flooded her mind. Her mouth formed a perfect little "O" as she recalled Ash's face buried in her bared breasts. With remembering last night's events in the bright of day, shyness swept over her, but her body had no problem responding to the memories of the vamp's cool kisses and exposed fangs taking blood from the side of her breast.

"Oh, Grammy," she murmured. "You were dead on right about vampires."

Up in a split second, she ran to the big mirror on the other side of the living room. She moved the dress down and pushed the bra to the side. She smiled in delight as she stroked the small bruise with two pinpricks on the side of her right breast. Seeing Ash's mark in such an intimate place made her thighs practically go up in flames.

She needed to shower and run errands but looked forward to possibly speaking to Ash later tonight while he was away in Denver. Surely, he would call when he woke up. She did a little sexy shimmy on her way to her bedroom. This would be the best, longest shower ever.

———

Ash adjusted his navy blue tie, brushing away a piece of lint from his black suit jacket. He didn't prefer suits, opting instead for his jeans, plain white T-shirt, and leather jacket but he knew he wore them well. He had left his casket in the dank cellar of the Saburova House in Denver over a half-hour ago to shower and dress. The cellar was the main storage place for expensive wines, but it had been renovated to include a large bathroom and made more comfortable for Ash's infrequent visits. An enforcer didn't sleep upstairs with the family, which suited him just fine. He planned to make this visit at Queen Galina's order as brief as possible.

Galina was, at the best of times, difficult and nearly intolerable to deal with and he often felt she was the only thing standing between him and a peaceful, if unfulfilling, existence as a vamp. She would be his queen for as long as he lived. He whispered her name a few times to himself, his lips moving into a grim, bitter little smile. Damn her. Damn himself for still wanting her after nearly ten decades.

Ash paused as he climbed the staircase that led from the cellar to the main house. He thought about Delilah for a few moments, remembering the look of passionate abandon on her beautiful face as he took blood from her breast the past night. He had taken careful little sips, stopping to steal glances at her face before gulping down her fragrant blood. His body tightened in reaction to the memory and he resolved to put Delilah out of his mind for good. He had settled the debt from one of his own vast accounts and that should have removed Declan from Galina's radar. Problem solved. He'd glamoured her brother after he left her place and that was the absolute end of it. His undead life as an enforcer for the queen and Vampire Council demanded zero distractions.

———

Delilah sighed and sipped her favorite herbal tea from the big brown mug. Just this morning, she had been excited to face the day ahead, confident that at some point after dusk she would hear from Ash. She glanced at the clock on the small table across from where she was seated on the sofa. It's been sundown for only a short while, she reasoned with herself.

To her great disappointment, she'd realized earlier in the afternoon that she didn't have Ash's number in her cell phone contacts. She had probably forgotten to put it in her new phone when she had bought it a few weeks before. Strange, she thought, her brow furrowing. She couldn't seem to recall a single digit of Ash's phone number. She took another sip of the hot tea, lost in thought?

She frowned. Her mind went back to last night. Ash had spoken in her ear softly that the debt was cleared, and she still had her bag filled with the five thousand dollars she'd offered him as payment. It was no surprise he hadn't taken her money and had resolved the situation. Ash was an old friend and had stepped in to help. She believed he genuinely cared about her and Declan's well-being. He seemed to be a good man, honest and forthright, but there was still that lingering thought to proceed with caution. *Ash handled everything, but what if it had been some other vampire?* Instinctively, Delilah knew Declan was traveling on a far darker path than even she had been aware of. It was time for the big sister to lay down the law again, which she fully intended to do with a phone call to Declan tonight. She checked her cell phone again.

———

Ash stood outside of the giant door of Galina's office, hand poised to knock. At his first rap, there was nothing but silence. He looked down the expansive hallway in both directions and a wave of annoyance filled him. The queen had arranged this meeting and the fact she apparently wasn't in her office signaled she was playing another one of her games with him. He resigned himself to simply wait her out.

Moments later, the heavy scent of roses filled his nose. He paused and turned around slowly. He knew the smell quite well and wasn't surprised to see Galina Saburova coming down the hallway.

Ash's glance took in her waterfall of smooth, straight blonde hair and the blue eyes bright with curiosity and amusement. She wore a simple black dress that fit her slim figure to perfection. As she approached, her perfume overwhelmed him. The sight and smell of her made him hard and he hated himself for it.

"Ash," she said, nodding. "Good to see you back here to do more of the Crown's necessary dirty work. I appreciate your promptness."

His eyes narrowed. "I'm here to do my job, yes."

"I can never wrap my head around why you don't just abandon your servitude to my empire and strike out on your own. There are many places where you could run to escape the Vampire Council and myself, of course." Galina's smile was small and mischievous.

"Ignore the Vampire Council's decision? I have many years of servitude left because I dared to kill another vampire. They spared my life and I do your dirty work on the sly." Ash's voice was even, devoid of any bitterness.

Galina tilted her head and held his gaze. "Was killing your maker worth it?"

Ash's lips curved in a half-smile. "I have no regrets every night when I wake up. I assumed we'd meet inside your office?"

The Queen barked an order. The door opened slowly to reveal two heavily armed guards, both vamps. Galina crossed the large, plush room and seated herself behind a large desk. The two guards took their positions on each side of the door they closed.

"Welcome back to my home, Ash," Galina said smoothly, not a trace of her Russian origins evident in her voice.

Ash nodded as he kept his face carefully blank. "Queen Galina, what do you need me to do?" Ash got right down to business, having no time for meaningless pleasantries. He knew the vampire queen expected nothing different from him. He was an enforcer, nothing more to many on the outside, though the situation was vastly more complicated than that. Concealed with civilized conversation, the two vamps were quietly and privately involved in a power struggle.

"My money is disappearing, which greatly upsets me." Galina drummed her fingers idly on her desk before continuing. "It's being siphoned out of two of my clubs, one here in Denver and one in Los Angeles. You will stop it from happening. Permanently."

Ash knew this would end in final deaths for the two groups of greedy vamps. When he was newly made, the thought of killing anyone was abhorrent to him but he was no longer that man. He killed to ensure his own survival and, in doing so, had made it an art he found satisfaction in. Killing humans was something he did rarely but destroying the vamps who preyed on them didn't keep him awake when he went to ground to sleep.

Galina gave Ash detailed instructions on how to handle the situations in Denver and Los Angeles before dismissing him abruptly. Ash left the office and the two armed guards closed the heavy door behind him. He pondered their exchange, sensing she would soon expect him to visit her bed. Nearly a hundred years was a long time to want a man but to desire as a vampire meant her twisted need for him would make her black and devious heart ache for him for an eternity. His lips twisted as he opened the front door and stepped outside. He liked the idea of it after the way she had used his love for her against him and discarded him for a horde of other lovers.

The black limousine waited for him outside of the large, sprawling Saburova home. Once he was seated inside, the driver exited the circular driveway, taking him to the private jet at the airport. Ash had a limited amount of time before he had to carry out Galina's orders. He knew exactly how to spend that time.

———

A few hours after sundown, Delilah was upset. As she brewed another steaming cup of tea, her mind swirled with a hundred different morbid possibilities of why Ash hadn't called her. She pictured another angry vamp driving a stake through his heart and her stomach dropped. As she knew all too well, sometimes bad things happen just as one was on the edge of being happy.

She had put on a new black bra and panty set underneath her black, lacy lounging gown, both of which she had bought that afternoon in one of the lingerie shops on the trendy Green Street. She wouldn't be sleeping with Ash tonight, but he had inspired her to just lie around and be sexy. She felt alive, vibrant, and gorgeous because of him. She hadn't felt this way in such a long time. Her last love affair break-up had sapped her of hope in settling down.

Delilah sat on the edge of her sofa, sipping her tea when the idea came to her. She could easily get Ash's phone number from Declan if he was around. It was also time to have that little talk with him. Her full lips curved into a pleased little smile at her ingenuity and she placed the cup down to grab her cellphone. The phone rang a few times before her brother picked up.

"Hey, De," Declan said, his voice booming. He sounded happy which was a welcome attitude adjustment from his sometimes surly demeanor. "How are you tonight?"

"I'm not very happy, Declan." She lowered her voice, clipping every word. "Your debt was nowhere near as small as five thousand dollars. You lied and if not for Ash, you would be in very serious trouble. Not ok, baby brother." Delilah took a deep breath before she continued in a cool tone of voice. "I've been taking care of you since you were sixteen and every year you seem to find a new way to wreck your life. And mine."

"Ash. Yeah, I saw him briefly last night. He told me the debt was settled, which I couldn't believe." Declan paused. "Did you sleep with him?"

"No, I didn't, not that it's any of your business," she snapped. "I know only a little about your underworld dealings, but I don't like it. That's Ash's world and we have no place in it. Go back to college and stay out of trouble, Declan. If you don't, help from me will be slow coming."

He huffed. "I will...soon. I'm young, De, and school is a big responsibility I honestly don't want to deal with right now. Don't worry. I'll get back in classes soon. No more gambling and creating big debts for me, ok? I won't waste this chance and bring you any more trouble."

"Thank you. I feel slightly relieved. By the way, I don't have Ash as a contact in my new phone. I need his cell phone number."

"I have his number right here in my phone. Just a sec, I'll text it to you, but take your own advice on this one—in case you're interested in him—stay out of Ash's vampire underworld. The undead can be ruthless. I know more than I probably should about it and I don't want to see you get hurt."

"I can handle myself with Ash, but thanks for caring."

Declan's text appeared on her phone screen and the conversation eased into quick small talk. She listened as he told her about his immense relief the big debt he owed had suddenly been taken care of and his plans for his new life. When she ended the call, Delilah rested her head back against the sofa and sighed with joy. She felt less stressed now that things seemed to be falling in place with her brother. Nervous butterflies darted around in her belly as she dialed Ash's number. When he didn't answer, she left him a voicemail she was sure he would respond to.

After waiting for a while with no call from him, Delilah hit the lights off in the living room, moving down the hallway to her bedroom. No response from Ash equaled a disappointing evening. As she changed into her sleeping gown, she calmed herself with soothing thoughts of Ash happily feeding and in perfect health. *He's fine wherever he is in Denver and he will call.*

Her lips curved in a small smile as her head hit the pillow.

————

Ash carefully brushed away the dirt from the simple gravestone that bore his father's name. *Andrew Lockler.* It had been a long time since he had thought about his father and even longer since he had visited his grave. On his knees in the small cemetery on the outskirts of Caddo, he looked back and forth at his parents' graves. *Sarah Lockler. I will never see them again in this life and probably not in the next.* His eyes watered unexpectedly, and a single, bloody tear trailed down his cheek. He brushed it away with the back of his hand but there was no shame in his crying.

Moonlight adorned the unkempt cemetery, giving it an unearthly, magical glow. Wrought iron gates stood sturdy and the large tree branches which hadn't been trimmed in years draped across several gravestones in the corner. He wasn't the only one guilty of not visiting his parents. As he stood, his cell phone vibrated. He ignored it, letting it go directly to voicemail without even pulling the cell out of his pocket.

Ash raised a hand to signal his driver that he was done. Headlights came on and the black limousine slowly approached the gates to the cemetery. He gave the graves one last look before walking away. It would probably be more than a few years before he came back to this place because he honestly couldn't stand the guilt of acknowledging what he was now. He was a predator when he had to be, nothing more. The time for reflection was over. The night hours were here, and it was time to feed.

————

Ash fell back against the seat in the limo, wiping the blood from his mouth with the back of his hand. His head pounded, and his stomach churned. He was drunk from taking in too much blood, too fast. He was having trouble seeing clearly, blearily making out the shape of the woman moving to embrace him. He pushed her away firmly and rapped on the partition glass. His driver knew what to do.

"Thank you for the feed, but no. I don't want to have sex with you." He spoke the words more sharply than he intended and she frowned. He struggled to remember her name as his head throbbed and, after a moment, recalled it. "Catherine, right? Thank you."

Catherine, a pretty, blonde groupie he had chosen to feed from for the evening, heaved an exaggerated, disappointed sigh and turned her pouting face to the window as the car sped along the dark interstate highway back to the city. "Fine. Whatever. I don't get turned down by vamps often."

Even the smaller towns like Caddo always had a vampire population and the inevitable, but scarce supply, of human groupies who were there to feed and sexually service them when needed. Some of the groupies with big mouths, like Catherine, had to be glamoured but most didn't. He knew what motivated all of them, the thrill that came with being so close to death and sexually mastered by beings that shouldn't even exist.

A few tense, silent moments later, the driver pulled up to the curb in front of a rundown apartment building in the crumbling, crime-ridden part of Caddo. Without hesitation, Ash took the vamp groupie's face in both hands, staring deeply into her eyes. Her eyes focused completely on his.

"Catherine, you won't remember anything about me. The only thing you will remember is you spent time with a vamp tonight and let him feed. There was no conversation about anything important. You never met this vamp before and you have no plans to see him again. Understand?"

Catherine nodded, her eyes still fixed on his.

Ash released her, rapping again on the glass. His driver opened the limo's back door a moment later, firmly escorting a dazed Catherine by the arm to the gate of her apartment building. Ash watched his driver place a thick envelope, filled with tens of thousands in cash, in her hand. Every human donor could live well for at least a year with the pay they received from vamps for their blood. The problem was many of them were groupies, not fit for the kind of exclusive arrangement he wanted. As they sped away, Ash's attention was caught by the sad decay of his old childhood neighborhood. Once, this part of Caddo had been thriving with beautiful, if small homes, sturdy trees, and lush grass.

He snorted aloud. This place was a fucking war zone now, taken over by the drug dealers and addicts. The prostitutes, though, were marginally better than the small group of vamp groupies, in his opinion. At least they weren't looking to flirt with death to get off.

He knew he had another twenty minutes before they'd reach the airport where the private jet would be waiting and ready to take him back to L.A. He had Galina's business to take care of there and Denver, of course, but the detour to Caddo was more important. He checked his phone, frowning at the unfamiliar number on the screen. Whoever it was had left a voicemail. He keyed in his password and tapped the screen to hear it.

Ash knew her voice right away and took in a deep breath he didn't need. Delilah McDade was speaking softly right in his ear, her voice sultry and a bit breathless. She sounded nervous but excited and the thought that he had made that kind of impact on such a quiet little mouse pleased him a little. She wanted to see him when he got back to L.A.

This was an unexpected tangle in his plan to never see her or deal with her brother again. Forcing himself to stop thinking about the problem of Delilah with his lower parts, he began thinking of possible ways to deal with the situation. Direct and firm rejection was probably best, but he didn't have the heart to break hers with a few, cruel words. He turned it over in his head for a few moments before the perfect plan came to him. *Just be yourself.* His lips twisted in a bitter smile.

His heart was heavy with the weight of old memories of who he used to be and fantasies of the man he should've grown to be. He closed his eyes against the onslaught.

Caddo, California, the past

Ash tilted his face to the midday sun, holding onto his big straw hat. The cool breeze had his bare arms tingling and the radiating warmth was welcome. He closed his eyes for a minute or two, lost in a daydream. He heard his Pa grunt loudly beside him and looked over to see he was holding out one of the old wooden rakes.

Ash grinned. "Sorry, Pa." He grabbed it and quickly began raking the golden brown and red leaves that had swirled down to the lush, soft bed of grass in their backyard. The long path embedded in the grass led to a simple red and brown brick house with a chimney on the roof and shutters on the windows.

Andrew Lockler was a tall, strapping man with a head full of greying blond hair. Ash had taken after his father's side of the family in just about every way. Physically, at least. He was more like his mother, Sarah, in personality—a dreamer. His Pa was more of a no-nonsense parent, who expected his only child to toe the line every step of the way.

He kept his gaze downward as he cleared his throat. "So, Pa, um…have you made up your mind about me going on the school field trip to the vineyards?"

Andrew's grunt was deeper this time. "Son, like I told you before, we just can't afford for you to go. Also, you have a new commitment this coming week. I'm going to have to keep you out of school for a couple of days. They added two new residential streets to my milk delivery route. I need your help."

Disappointment stung in Ash's gut. No class field trip meant no kissing fun with Marian, a particularly loose redheaded girl he'd been having fun with occasionally. And, he had to work with his Pa? It just kept getting worse. He heaved a sigh. "Pa, but what…what if I could pay for everything myself and even give you a little to help you and Ma out with the groceries?"

Andrew stopped raking, fixing his narrowed eyes on Ash. "How would you do that, son?"

Ash dropped the rake and dug into his pants pocket. He slowly pulled out a crisp, folded ten dollar bill and held it up. "With this."

His Pa moved to stand in front of him. At seventeen, Ash was muscular, but he still had some growing to do to catch up to his father.

"Where'd you get that kind of money? I know you would never steal from me and your mother. So, where?"

Ash shrugged casually as his heart thumped in his chest. "I found it."

Andrew wiped his sweaty brow with his forearm, sighing deeply. "Where exactly did you find a ten dollar bill? Outside or inside of whose store?"

Relenting, Ash looked into his father's eyes. He would rather tell the truth than have his Pa believe he'd stolen the money from one of the hardworking shop owners. He struggled to keep his voice even. "I got into a fight with Burt and swiped it from his pocket after I beat the—"

"The Evans boy? You stole money from him after you fought with him?"

His Pa's tone had him looking away guiltily. "Yes, Pa." His eyes were defiant when he looked up again. "He was taunting me, saying I was a pansy and I couldn't take him. Well, I did. I whooped him good."

Andrew's hand rested heavily on his shoulder. "I don't care that he provoked you. He's two years and fifty pounds behind you. It wasn't a fair fight and you made things even worse by stealing from him."

"But, Pa, you're always saying that sometimes a real man has to fight to protect his honor."

"This wasn't about honor, Asher. There's nothing honorable about what you've done. I taught you to stand up for what you believe in that is good and true and to defend that. This was just theft." He snatched the bill from his son's hands.

"That money could help us out with the groceries!"

His Pa's eyes glinted in the sun as he clenched his jaw. "We don't need stolen money just like we don't need handouts. A real man accepts neither. I want you to be a good man, upright and proud. I didn't raise a coward, a bully, and a thief."

Ash looked at the grass, deeply ashamed. He had never done anything like this before and, with the way Pa had him feeling, he knew he never would again. "Yes, Pa. I'll, um, return the money to Burt."

To his surprise, Andrew clapped him soundly on the back. "That's the good, young man I know." He gestured at the scattered leaves. "Finish this *task and get on over to the Evans' house before lunch. Your Ma will be expecting you back on time."*

Ash murmured, "Yes, sir" to his Pa's retreating back and started raking.

Ash's lips slashed in a grim smile as the limousine rolled on into the night. He thanked a God he wasn't even sure he believed in that his parents had been spared knowing the kind of man he'd become. On some days, he was a calculating bastard and on others, he was a greedy vampire's worst nightmare. His jaw clenched. Damn Galina for demanding his involvement in bullshit like this. He hated vamp politics and did all he could to avoid them, but he was the best enforcer the vamp world had seen in decades. He would keep cleaning up his queen's messes as long as the Crown demanded it. The silent part of him he kept buried deep in his heart was a still a dreamer and he dreamed to be free.

———

"You're gonna pay for this, Lockler," the vamp snarled, even as Ash tightened the pressure on the hold he had of the man's neck. "You and Saburova will fucking pay when my associates hear about this."

Ash reached deep in the pocket of his leather jacket for his trusty wood stake. "Maybe, but they won't hear about it from you. Ever." Ash drove the stake deep into the vamp's chest, satisfied when the body crumbled before completely exploding into dust. He brushed the dust from his jacket and returned the stake to his pocket.

He looked around the back room of the Los Angeles nightclub, taking in the dusty piles of vampire carnage scattered on the floor. He would handle the same sort of business in Denver to finish his task as the queen's enforcer. He had no fear of the eternal death for vamps and that's what made him good at what he did.

Ash left the room of the club through the back exit and slid into limousine that waited for him. His next order of business, once his driver dropped him off at his place, was to deal with the lovely Delilah.

Later, when he was settled in at home, he pulled up her phone number on his cell. After a few rings, Delilah's sleepy voice was in his ear. "Hello?"

"Delilah," he answered smoothly. "I must have disturbed your sleep. I would've called at some other time, but I really needed to speak with you."

"Ash, it's fine. I haven't heard from you and I...I was worried."

"I appreciate your concern." He paused for a brief moment. "I'm back in L.A. and I want to see you. I'll pick you up at your place tomorrow night at eight. Wear something black and snug."

She sounded fully awake, her tone laced with honey. "Oh, that won't be a problem. I'm, um, excited to be seeing you."

"Good. I'll see you then. Sleep tight, sweet Delilah."

"I will. Good night, Ash." He put his cell back on the nightstand. He hadn't forgotten her pretty face, soft skin, and lush body, though he knew he should. He lay in the dark for long moments, deeply contemplating his next move with her.

———

Delilah checked her reflection in the long bedroom mirror and fixed a smear of lip gloss. She turned around, looking at every angle with a smile and was finally satisfied that her tight black dress and matching heels would be enough to make Ash hungry for her. She wore her normally curly halo of hair straight, the sleek waterfall gliding down her back. She was excited, aroused, and ready for whatever pleasure the night would bring.

Just as she flipped off the light switch, the doorbell rang. She heaved a deep, nervous sigh, heading to answer it. She opened the door slowly and her lips curved in a smile. Ash stood there, handsome in his dark suit. He gave her a slow, thorough once over from her hair down to her heeled feet. His smile was sinful, full of dark, sensual promise.

"You're breathtaking, Delilah. You surpass my expectations by a country mile." He inclined his head. "Lock up your place and let's have a little fun tonight."

"Thank you. I wanted to look my best for you." Delilah grabbed her clutch purse from the table before locking the door from the inside and closing it. She was slightly unsteady on her feet as they walked down the path from her condo and Ash put a hand on the curve of her back, guiding her to the black Lexus parked on the street. Her body brushed against his and she enjoyed every moment of the contact. He unlocked his car with a click of his remote, helping her in.

She spoke when he was seated inside. "What do you have planned for us?"

He gave her a hot look. "It's so much better to show you rather than tell you."

She bit back a ton of questions she wanted to ask, remaining as silent as he was during the car ride. She trembled with nerves, her hands tightly clasped in her lap. Soon they arrived at their destination, he parked the car and went around to open the door for her. The parking lot was well lit, and she focused on his face. She returned the small smile he gave her as he grasped her hand and led her to the front entrance of a club.

"This is an exclusive vamp club. Human guests are permitted, though they're rarely here. Don't stray from my side. I don't want someone else to think you're here for the taking."

Delilah nodded, drinking in the sights and sounds of the place. The night club was far more lavish than any other she had been in. It was dim, the lighting giving it an atmospheric touch. Private, black leather booths lined the chrome walls all around with a small dance floor in the center. Ash took her hand and led her to a back booth.

As they sat down, she noticed more than a few men, no doubt vamps, glancing in their direction. Slightly uncomfortable but happy to be spending the evening with him, she shrugged off her shyness, squeezing his hand for a brief moment. "What do they serve here for you? Blood only, I imagine?"

"Blood tinged alcoholic drinks. Vamps can eat and drink but most of us prefer not to. I still like my hard liquor."

He called a server over and ordered them both drinks before turning his gaze back to her. "We'll start here and move to the back room later."

"What's in the back room?"

He smiled, stroking her cheek with his fingers. "Something you shouldn't miss, sweet Delilah."

———

Ash's dancing was a study in seduction, every movement of his thighs pressed against her, making Delilah shiver. She could feel him hard and erect against her belly. They moved together on the dancefloor to the slow music and he held her tightly to him. Her head rested against his neck and she sniffed his cologne.

"You smell heavenly." His voice was rough. "It's taking everything in me not to take you hard and fast in the back of my car right now."

Delilah's pulse raced. "I'm not confident that I could say no to that."

He broke away from her, grabbed her hand, and led her to the back of the club. "I want to show you what happens in this room." He opened the door for her,

She stepped inside, not sure if what she was seeing was really happening. All around the room, in various positions, were couples having sex. Her lips slightly parted in shock and she looked at Ash. His expression was difficult to read as his eyes bored into hers. A woman with dark hair, dressed seductively in a red dress, approached them. She flashed her fangs, reaching up to cup Ash's face in her hands.

"I haven't seen you in months. Every night that you're not here ends in disappointment for me." She gave Delilah a dismissive glance. "I see you've brought a human playmate with you."

Ash spoke smoothly. "Anabelle, I've been busy but thinking of you." He stepped in front of Delilah and grabbed the female vamp in his embrace. His lips traveled from her ear down to the tops of her breasts as she laughed. "Yes, this is my human plaything for the evening." He winked at Delilah.

Her heart dropped, and her stomach twisted in knots as tears sprang to her eyes. "I-I don't understand. What is all this?"

Ash slapped the vamp's ass, sending her off with a whisper in her ear. "Not yet, but you will. This, sweet Delilah, is a place for vamps to indulge in every sexual delight with both other vamps and willing humans. You have a body made for sin and I want to explore it tonight somewhere that makes me feel comfortable." He grabbed her around the waist, grinding his erection into her. He nipped her ear and she fiercely pushed him off.

"If you think you can talk me into having sex with you in a room full of people, you're crazy." Her teary eyes flashed angrily, and she spoke through gritted teeth. "I'm grabbing my purse and I'm leaving right this minute. I don't want to interrupt your good time, so I'll call a cab, you bastard."

She left him standing as she dashed through the door. She stopped long enough to grab her small bag and headed out the front door of the nightclub. As the chilly winter air hit her face, she sucked down gulps of it. She tried to think clearly. She was working purely on instinct as she pulled out her cell phone.

In the next moment, Ash was standing in front of her, his face stony. "You said you wanted to know all about my life and I've shown you. Whatever romantic dreams you had about me were your own misconceptions." He took her chin in his hand. "I like to fuck, Delilah. The hotter and dirtier, the better. That's who I am."

She slapped his hand away and brushed the tears from her cheeks. "Oh, God! I'm not into all this. Your lifestyle is not for me. You're right. This was all my own mistake. Just take me home, Ash. Now."

He took her arm, pulling her in the direction of the parking lot. "Fine. Let's go."

———

Delilah sat next to him in the car on the drive to her home, her body a tense bundle of nerves. The silence was palpable, and he frequently looked at her profile as she stared straight ahead. Once they arrived, he escorted her to her front door, still quiet.

Her hands shook as she dug through her bag for the keyring, keeping her eyes lowered as Ash stood next to her. She hadn't expected her dream evening with him to go so horribly wrong. She turned the key in the lock and stepped inside. "Thank you for seeing me home. Goodbye." She went to close the door in his face, but he blocked it with his hand.

"Delilah, look—"

She flipped on the porch light so that she could see his face clearly. She raised her chin. "Whatever you're going to say, save it. I fully acknowledge my part in this mess. I shouldn't have tried to seduce you. The way you live—I don't swing that way. Thanks for not pushing the issue. One question though, why did you clear the debt in exchange for only a little of my blood and no sex? A hundred thousand dollars is not exactly pocket change."

His face was blank, and his words were measured. "It is to me. The last thing you and your brother needed was to owe money to the vampire queen, and I shouldn't have blindsided you like that at the club. The kind of woman you are…I should've known you couldn't handle the way I live." He ran his hand through his hair. "I'm guessing we shouldn't talk to each other again."

"I'll be your extended friend from a safe distance because of Declan, of course."

Ash nodded. "Of course." He offered his hand. "Are we parting as friends?"

Delilah hesitated, putting her hand in his. "Friends, it is."

He held on tightly for a few long, awkward moments. "Listen, that great, loving human guy is out there for you and I'm sure he'll give you the world. All I can offer is no strings sex and you obviously are worth so much more." His lips curved in a smile. "Stop fantasizing so much about the damned undead and let him find you." He brushed the back of her hand with his lips and her body tingled all over. "Goodnight, sweet Delilah."

He was striding down the path before she could say another word, which was probably for the best. Her heart was still pounding in excitement at being so close to him. Her response to him made her wonder if she would've invited him into her bed if he had pressed her. Her heart cried for him as she closed the door, leaning back against it with her eyes closed. *What's done is done. Time to move on, girl.*

THREE

Ash tapped his cell phone screen, saving the voicemail he had listened to from William Watts, one of the elder members of the Vampire Council. His mind was spinning with the possibilities of what he wanted to discuss. The elder had been a key member of the council over a hundred years before Ash had been turned. He genuinely liked him and respected his wisdom, which he couldn't say about many vamps.

He leaned back in his black recliner, dressed only in a pair of old faded jeans, and felt the troubling emptiness of a life led in solitude. After his disastrous affair with Galina, he had sworn off love and contented himself with warm, giving, beautiful bodies for sex and occasional blood donations. *Contented? Hardly.* He grimaced as thoughts of the lovely Delilah assailed him once again, as they had since that last night with her two days ago. It pained him to admit his plan to set her free from him and his dangerous life had caught him in his own trap. She probably hated his fucking guts and he still desired her, now possibly even more for the way she had taken him down a notch that night at the vamp club. After the way he treated her, he felt lower than a dog's ass for hurting her intentionally.

His stomach rumbled, and he looked out the balcony sliding glass doors as dusk was surrendering to nightfall. The urge to feed was particularly strong tonight and he stood up to go dress himself. He needed a human blood donor and, just maybe, some sex to take his mind off the one woman he would never possess, in bed or otherwise. Delilah's beautiful face flashed in his mind, his thoughts turning to the fullness of her lips, her soft skin, and the roundness of her curves. Her heart beat with a goodness he had never known from the women in his life, except his beloved mother. *Best to let her live her life without me anywhere in it.*

————

Delilah shut down her work station PC and sighed at the lateness of the hour. This day had been anything but productive, but she knew the leftover work could be done at home. She had wanted this position with KinderFun but still was less than thrilled at the mass amounts of overtime required from her in exchange for a high salary. She glanced at the large bouquet of deep crimson roses in a black decorative vase on her desk. They had come earlier that day, much to her surprise. The small white card read simply, "I'm Sorry." She was instantly high on emotion, thoughts of Ash sending them making her heart beat a little faster. She yanked herself down just as quickly, knowing if he had sent them, he probably felt guilty for playing around with Declan's sister. It wasn't a declaration of undying love. It wasn't an invitation to be in his life. It was nothing but a standard apology and she would treat it as such.

Her co-worker, David, popped his head in her cubicle with a smile. "I'm shutting everything down for the evening, too. Do you need help getting that gorgeous bunch of roses in your car?"

Delilah smiled in return, nodding. "Yes, that would be great."

David cleared his throat meaningfully. "I couldn't help but notice the card. If those roses are any indication, this guy's really sorry. If it's not your brother, I say forgive and forget. You need some love in your world. Hell, we all do. This one might be a keeper."

She couldn't help but laugh. "Oh, it's complicated but I'll keep your advice in mind."

Together, they shut down the office and she slipped on her heavy black coat, swung her purse strap over her shoulder, and grabbed her laptop. David held the heavy flower vase with both hands and they headed out to the employee parking lot.

Ash watched Delilah emerge from her office building with another man. His eyes narrowed and focused intently. He sat in his car, a safe distance in the darkness, as he had been since dusk. He noted in satisfaction that she hadn't angrily dumped his roses but was a bit concerned about the man with her. He immediately dismissed the thought that she was dating him. *Probably just a co-worker.* He didn't stop to assess why he cared so much. He chalked the gesture up to a nice, sincere apology and that was the end of it. It had been two days of, not just sexual longing for her, but a deeper feeling of wanting to simply talk with her in that easy, familiar way they had on the first night when he had glamoured her. The whole glamouring process could be tricky—it made most people completely compliant and with others it only gave a slight mental nudge to do his bidding. Delilah was clearly one of the latter, as she had maintained enough of her own free will to push him out of her life. He had a deep fear of what may come if she ever woke up from it, which given her mental strength, could possibly happen at any time. *House of cards, he mused.* He knew her well enough to know if she was cold now, she'd be frostier than an Alaskan winter if she knew he was never an old friend. He would see her home safely tonight and then stay away and simply fade out her life.

Comfortable on her living room sofa in pink shorty pajamas, Delilah sipped a soothing cup of chamomile tea. The TV volume was low as the rainfall tapped in rhythm against her windows and thunder rumbling. She adored thunderstorms, so she was pleased that one had hit Los Angeles tremendously hard this evening.

She struggled to keep her mind off Ash but since he'd sent the roses, everything about him filled her head with silly visions of the way things could've been. *If he could be satisfied with just me, maybe.* She still felt the sting of jealousy remembering his hands and lips all over the luscious Anabelle. It felt unfair that the vamp was a part of his hedonistic life, even though that wasn't her thing.

She jumped from a loud clatter outside. Thunder crackled, and lightning illuminated her back porch. She flipped on the porch light and peered out the glass patio door, watching through the cracks in the blinds. Her heart thumped in her chest as she realized two men were struggling in a fight outside. She stayed very still, trying to make out who was there. She was about to grab her phone to call 911 before she recognized Ash, soaked in his leather jacket, straddling another man and punching him repeatedly in the face.

She unlocked and slid the door back and stepped out. She backed up at the look on Ash's face as he spotted her. "Get the hell back inside. Now." His voice was a growl.

The other man took advantage of the break in the blows to his face and gained the upper hand. Shoving Ash off and back into the rose planter, he darted to the back of the yard, easily leaping the tall wooden fence.

Ash got to his feet slowly, hands on his knees, not looking at her. When he straightened up, she could see the bruises already forming on his face, his lower lip bloodied. He walked towards her and she backed up a bit as he stepped inside. His blond hair was plastered to his head, his green eyes piercing as he looked her over.

"I imagine you wouldn't let a stranger in and maybe I shouldn't be an exception."

She cleared her throat nervously. "I trust you…to a point. What just happened? What in hell were you doing out there?"

He shrugged off his black leather jacket before answering, draping it over a nearby chair. When he turned back to her, his gaze was penetrating, and she suddenly felt vulnerable in her skimpy pajama shorts. "I'm trying to protect you. That vamp was outside on your patio, watching you."

Delilah sucked in a sharp breath and her stomach churned in fear. "Does this have something to do with Declan's debt and his underworld connections?"

Ash nodded. "It could. I settled your brother's debt, as promised. However, the word must be out that he has a sister and some player in the underworld may have developed an interest in you. Don't worry. You and your brother are safe. I'll handle this, too."

She stood in front of him, lightly touching the bruises on his face. "Thank you for protecting us. Stay right there. I'm going to grab some gauze and antiseptic to clean you up."

Grabbing up the things she needed from the bathroom, she padded down the hallway to find him still standing in the same spot. She gestured at the high stool at the granite topped bar and he sat down.

Moments passed in silence as she moistened pieces of gauze and gently cleansed the wounds on his jaw and bottom lip. She worked in silence, ignoring his gaze intently focused on her face. "Any human guy would be swearing a blue streak in pain, but this doesn't seem to hurt you at all."

"I can handle a lot of pain. This is nothing. I'll heal in a few hours, but thanks for cleaning me up. I know I'm not your favorite person right now."

Delilah shrugged lightly and taped the gauze to the scraped and bruised area beneath his eye. "It's really no big deal."

"You do realize that in dealing with underworld players, your brother has probably endangered you both, right?"

She nodded and stepped back after she finished. "He promised me this was his last big mistake and he was at least considering returning to college. I think he really means it this time. He knows the importance of succeeding in school because I've pounded it into him for the past five years, just like our Mom did before she passed away." She rolled her eyes. "Plus, he knows if he doesn't abandon this lifestyle, I'll be forced to cut him off financially. Believe it, that's quite a motivator for him."

"I know a little about your family ties, about how you and your brother were raised by your mom and your grandma, after your dad apparently abandoned you." He shook his head slowly. "I feel it's best to tell you the absolute truth about that whole situation. I knew your father, Martin."

Delilah's eyes widened. "How did you know him?

"You know your dad also had underworld dealings, I'm assuming?"

She nodded. "Our grandma shared her suspicions with us about his involvement. She never believed in keeping secrets when it came to him. She insisted he hadn't just run off but probably caught a bullet instead." She drew in a shaky breath. "I'm not even sure if I want to hear what you have to tell me." She met his eyes, with tears in her own. "Ash, where is my dad?"

His expression was somber as he spoke softly. "I only met him a few times in passing but I knew all about his money troubles. I also knew he had a family. Martin was a bit player in a game he never had a chance in Hell of winning. He couldn't pay his off his massive debts which annoyed the vampire queen, Galina. She had him erased by one of her enforcers, honey. I wasn't a part of it, wasn't even there when it happened, but I know for sure he's dead. I don't know where he's buried. If I did, I wouldn't keep that from you. I'm sorry you don't have any idea where to take flowers and grieve in peace."

Twin trails of tears streamed down her cheeks and a little sob escaped her throat as she dashed them away. He moved from the bar stool, fiercely jerking her into his embrace and kissing her forehead. She wasn't surprised by Ash's revelation, long believing her grandmother's suspicions, but to hear her father's death as a reality was still painful. Her mind was spinning, fear gripping her as she thought about Declan's association with the same underworld that had taken their father.

"Thank you for telling me the truth. Dad disappeared when Declan was barely old enough to understand the significance of it. He's had a good life with a proper upbringing but still being without a father impacted him. I had to grow up quickly to help my Mom take care of us and I've always had a hand in raising him."

Ash gently took her chin in his hand. "I don't want to see your brother become another casualty of the violence I'm forced to deal with every day. That's exactly what will happen if he continues down this road he's on. I can only protect him to a certain point." He paused, keeping his gaze locked with hers. "You need to know —I've claimed you as my property, under our laws in the vampire kingdom. You and your brother have my protection."

Delilah kept her eyes downcast, speaking softly. "I'm starting to get tough with him, which is exactly what he needs. Thank you for keeping us safe." He stroked her cheek. "I think I understand you and your family dynamics a little better now. You became a responsible caretaker at a young age. Bless your tender heart, honey. This is why you're so cool and collected, on the surface, anyway." His eyes bored into hers. "When have you ever taken time to live for just you, sweet Delilah?"

Her voice was calm and even, but her pulse raced in excitement at his touch. "I don't have time to think of only myself. I never have."

She looked away to the vase of roses he had sent to her office. Her gaze darted back to him. "Thank you for the roses. That was very thoughtful."

"You're very welcome." His tone was amused, and a small smile played on his lips. "I owed you a big apology. I've been drinking tonight – all night. Can you guess why, Delilah?"

She tried to back away, but he caught her around the waist and held her captive against his damp, leanly muscled body. She fought weakly for a moment before resigning herself to standing still as he looked down at her. "I don't know your life, Ash. Women troubles?" Her tone was snappish, as if she didn't give a damn but she was more than interested.

He shook his head slowly. "One woman. You. I was a complete ass that last night on purpose and I sent you the roses to tell you I'm sorry for that. It was necessary, in a way you may never fully understand. My life…" He heaved a deep sigh. "…would only hurt you and possibly even get you killed. None of my performance at the club was real. Well, not anymore. I used to live just like that and that recklessness and little regard for decency will always be a part of me."

Delilah trembled as he held her, her heart pounding. She cautiously raised a hand to brush strands of his wet hair from his face. "Why would you do that to me? Do you mean you put on that act to keep me safe? From what exactly?" She licked her lips and his eyes tracked the movement.

"My life is dangerous and there are countless other vamps in our underworld who would see you as the easiest target for a way to get to me. I was a selfish bastard to ever involve myself with you. I should've left you alone the first night we met." He ran his thumb across her full lips, parting them. "I just wanted a taste of you, honey. Just like I do right now."

He lowered his head and his lips settled on hers as his tongue slipped inside. He tasted like liquor and sweetness she had been too long denied. He broke the kiss to run his tongue from the shell of her ear down her neck and the dam broke inside of her. She dragged his head back and kissed him with abandon. His tongue played with hers, as his hands traveled the length of her body. He pushed her back against the wall and continued his gentle assault on her senses.

His kisses kept coming as his hands slid beneath her tank top, cupping her full breasts. She gasped as his fingers played with her hardened nipples before pulling the top over her head to expose her to his hot gaze. He lowered his head, nibbling the undersides of her breasts before his tongue teased her sensitive tips. Delilah clutched his broad shoulders, fighting for air as she was caught up in a maelstrom of sensation.

"So damn beautiful," he murmured.

Delilah weakly tried to move his mouth from her. "This is not a good idea." Her voice was breathy. "Maybe we should… oh!...stop!" He gently suckled her nipples and she felt herself losing control, her common sense eluding her.

He jerked back, and his eyes bored into hers. "If you tell me to stop and mean it, I'll go away and never darken your door again. There are a thousand reasons we shouldn't do this, but I can't think of single one right now. Can you?" His thumb brushed across the sensitive tip of one breast and she squirmed in pleasure.

Her fingers played in his hair for a moment before she slowly shook her head. "I can't think at all. Please don't stop, Ash."

He nodded and kissed her neck as his hands slid inside of her shorts. He traced the rim of her black lace panties. She groaned low in her throat as his fingers teased her moistening pussy. She parted her legs and he rested his body between them, finding her bud and playing with it until she gasped loudly in the silence.

Wanting him to burn like she was, she slid her hands beneath his black T-shirt and caressed his muscled chest. She reached down and deftly unzipped him, cupping his hard cock in her hands. She toyed with the tip, lightly circling it with her fingertips before sliding down the shaft. His light moans against her neck spurred her on and she boldly gripped him firmly.

Ash went down on his knees in front of her, tugging her shorts and panties off. He gave her a grin. "I've always wanted to see your undies." He draped one of her legs across his shoulder, exposing her pussy to him. His tongue started at her belly, moving in circles before he slid it deep in her warm softness. Delilah let out a tortured scream as he licked her, teasing her bud with the tip of his tongue before sliding it deep inside again. She held on to his shoulder with one hand, leaning back against the wall to keep from sliding down, weak from the way he pleasured her.

He grabbed her around her hips, dragged her down to the carpet with him, and rolled her naked body beneath him. He spread her legs and fit his body between them. He met her eyes as she ground her hips against him. "Last chance, Delilah. Please don't tease. My control is not so good tonight. Do you want this?" Every word he spoke was soft and deliberate.

She kissed his neck, taking his cock and rubbing it against her softness. "God, yes."

He positioned himself, sliding deep into her warm sheath with a sigh. Cradling her hips in his hands, his gaze focused intently on her as she took all of him. Her eyes narrowed, and she groaned when he lightly thrust deeper, filling her completely. She grasped his ass with both hands, guiding him in a rhythm that pleased her.

The rain fell against the windows in sheets, thunder rumbling as the lightning crackled and flashed. The ferocity of the storm outside mirrored the passion they shared as he steadily moved inside of her, whispering sweet words of desire in her ear. "Sweet like sugar. Don't hold back from me. I want to see you come apart for me."

She wrapped her legs around his waist, whispering her pleasure to him in his ear over and over. She was so very close to coming but fought it back. She never wanted their love making to end. He tormented her sensitive bud with his fingers and she exploded from his intimate touch, her orgasm coming in waves. He continued to thrust for long moments before he spilled himself inside of her, shouting a loud curse word.

He stayed there on top of her, brushing her hair back from her face with a satisfied smile. He rested his forehead in the crook of her neck as she struggled to breathe in deeply. She cradled his head with one hand, still trying to come to grips with the fact that she and Ash had just had mind blowing sex for the first time and it was every bit as good as she had imagined.

Delilah woke up on her floor in darkness, the rain steadily pelting her windows in the silence. She stayed completely still, confused as to why she was lying in a man's embrace. She still had tangled dream images in her mind and she struggled to remember. She had been at Vivian's and she was talking with a man with blond hair in a booth. She recalled being extremely upset. Like a floodgate opening, the memories rushed back. Ash Lockler wasn't a vamp who was a long dear friend. He wasn't anything but someone Declan owed thousands of dollars.

She scrambled to turn around in the man's arms and, just as she suspected, it was Ash she was cuddled with. Nude. Completely bare-assed. She angrily shoved him away as he tried to pull her back, moving as quickly as she could in the dark to find her pajamas. She quickly dressed and flipped on a lamp. With narrowed eyes, she landed blows on his chest and shoulders. "You lowdown, lying bastard! You wiped my mind clean and took full advantage of me and the situation."

His gaze was direct and unflinching as he grabbed her arms. "You remember it all now? I did glamour you, but I never took advantage of you. You were more than an active participant when we had sex tonight. You can't blame that on me 'wiping your mind clean'. Glamouring doesn't work that way. Yes, I lied but it was necessary, and I never imagined things would go this far." He ran a hand through his hair. "I honestly came to check on you and nothing more. I'm very sorry you feel manipulated."

"Oh, I definitely feel that, Mr. Lockler. Also, add to it used and seduced by a master." She wrenched away from him, fighting the tears welling in her yes. "That first night you said you wanted my body. Well, now that you've helped yourself to it, you can get the fuck out." Her anger raised a notch at the smile tugging at his lips. She pointed at the front door. "Move it! I don't see you leaving fast enough."

"There's that fire I sensed in you from our first meeting. Your coldness is intriguing, but your fire is irresistibly hot." He raised his jeans zipper and grabbed his leather jacket from the chair. "Go on and hate me, if it soothes you. I don't regret owning you for just tonight and I will honor the agreement I made with you regarding Declan. The debt is paid so it's a non-issue."

"You bet your ass the debt is settled. Too bad I had to screw you to do it." She dashed falling tears away. "You said you're no longer that man you were at the vamp club." She raised her chin defiantly and hissed her words at him. "I don't believe that for a second. You're a manipulator I don't ever want to see again in this lifetime."

On his way to the front door, he caught her around the waist, dragging her to him. "Too bad that's not the way this works. I've endangered you and your brother by mere association. Tonight proved that, so I'll remain in your life for at least a few more weeks to protect you."

Delilah snorted. "That's like the wolf guarding the hen house with a mouth full of feathers. We don't need your protection, Mr. Lockler. I could never trust you the way I did when you had me spun out of my mind."

His voice clipped each word as he dressed himself. "This is not a game. I have no further reason to lie to you. If I say it's dangerous for you to know me at all, believe me. When I'm satisfied that you're both safe, I'll leave you alone." He released her and strode to the front door. As he turned the knob, he gave her one last look. "I'll be around. You won't see me, but I'll be right there."

The door closed firmly, and Delilah grabbed a throw pillow, punching it. The anger was slowly giving way to shame and the only thing she wanted to do at that moment was bury herself in her bedcovers.

FOUR

Galina quickly read the text message on her cell phone, frowning darkly, before she flung it across the room. She had Ash under surveillance and the news about the human woman he had taken up with infuriated her. Her intel-servants noted that he had left the woman's home just a few minutes before. She knew well enough that Ash visiting any woman in the wee hours of the morning meant he was screwing her. She dug her nails into her hand in frustration.

What they had shared years ago was over, the fire long extinguished, by his choice. *But, what if I can get him back?* She needed a way to keep him under her thumb and out of the arms of any other woman, human or otherwise. To own Ash again, with him holding her in the darkness after she had just ridden him thoroughly, was the only thing that made her existence without a real lover tolerable. Getting Ash back under her control was the only thing that made sense. She would make him see how good they were together.

She smiled coolly, the beginnings of a plan turning over in her mind. Ash was always one step from being rebellious and he needed to be handled in a way that ensured he stayed in line. With a new human playmate, he seemed to be strangely attached to, the best way to control him could possibly be to control his woman.

The memories of how she and Ash had been once upon a time burned in her gut. Her hands clenched in fists, the nails digging in deeply. She barely noticed the pain, her mind lost in the past.

Denver, Colorado, the past

The large cathedral was empty except for Galina, the hushed silence weighted with the anguish of those left behind to mourn the dead. The raindrops pelted the ornate stained-glass windows and jasmine coming from the decorative scent pots wafted in the air. She stood with her back ramrod straight in a short black dress and high heels, a short lace veil covering her eyes. She closed her eyes for a moment at the enormity of it all, smiling. Her finger traced the ornate trails of pure gold on the large urn set to the side of the altar.

"So, this is your end, my powerful King Dmitri." She chuckled. "I told you I would eventually win. I always do. Ash will, once again, be melting your ice queen tonight."

Her razor-sharp hearing detected footsteps long before the cathedral doors opened, and a gust of freezing wind blew in. Two figures emerged from the darkness of the large hall, into the sanctuary. She nodded at Ash as he took a seat on a pew at the very back. He knew his place was not at her side at this moment and he respected that.

The second figure strutted up the red carpeted aisle, also in a short black dress and matching high heels. Galina's eyes narrowed as she recognized one of her dead husband's whores. There were so many she had stopped counting decades ago. She inclined her head slightly at the tall, slim vamp with a pixie haircut and smooth ebony skin.

"I see you've come to pay your respects, Chyna." Galina carefully kept her voice devoid of any emotion.

Chyna's eyes slitted. "Is that what this farce of a memorial service was supposed to be about? Paying respects? That's hilarious coming from you. You had no respect for Dmitri in life and even less now that he's dead."

Galina's eyes may have glimmered with hate, but her face remained impassive. "What in the hell are you spouting?" she demanded and went immediately on guard, tensing as Chyna moved closer.

"I know all about your affair with Ash Lockler," Chyna hissed. "I know Dmitri wanted it ended. He was prepared to take the knowledge of your dirty dealings to the Vampire Council. That's why you drove a stake through his heart."

"It was more like a sharpened bit of ivory tusk through the back," Galina murmured. "He had his affairs and I had mine. Hardly a reason to kill him, considering I control the council."

"You admit it!" Chyna burst out.

"I admit nothing." Her eyes narrowed. "Be very careful about those accusations. I am still your queen."

Chyna snorted. "Aren't we vamps suffering because you wear the crown? I'm not afraid of you."

Galina's laughter tinkled in the heavy silence. She reached into the urn with one finger. In a split second, she had the other vamp in a headlock, wiping the grey ash onto her forehead. "This, you stupid bitch, is all that's left of your precious Dmitri and his dreams of taking over my empire. He forgot that I am queen and I made him my king." She noted Ash coming down the aisle and released Chyna.

Ash stood at the foot of the small steps leading up to the altar. "My Queen, the weather is getting pretty fierce. We should really be on our way." Amusement laced his tone.

Galina nodded, stepped down, and took Ash's outstretched hand. His smile was lazy with passion that had been tamped down all evening and a flush of arousal shot through her. The annoying scene with the gnat, Chyna, was swiftly forgotten as they walked down the aisle and out the front doors.

———

Galina groaned deep in her throat. Knowing that some little nobody human bitch was screwing Ash the way she used to left her feeling hollow. Her countless other lovers meant nothing now that there may be a shadow of a chance of recapturing his heart, mind, and trust. She would never make the disastrous mistake of marrying again. She didn't care that Ash had no formal royal title and had no qualms about being seen with him in polite vamp society. She was content to let them all speculate. All she cared about was having him back in her bed and back under her total control, no matter the cost. *Now, if I can make my plans for Little Nobody Bitch a reality.*

———

Delilah kept steady pace with the traffic in her little white Volkswagen Beetle. Her mind contemplated possibilities a million miles away as she drove to have an early dinner with her close friend, Mari. The sun was setting low in the west, casting vibrant orange and deep red shadows. She slid her shades on, lowering the visor.

Damn Ash Lockler. She couldn't forget how he had maneuvered his way into her life. She also couldn't forget his brand of loving. She crinkled her nose in annoyance at herself as her body tingled in remembrance. She was pretty much over the initial shock and embarrassment of being so wanton with him, but she still had plenty of fiery curse words to fling at him if she ever saw his face again. *But, he is protecting me and Declan.* He wasn't all bad but still a real life, larger than fiction vampire. She knew well enough that she had no business tangling with the undead.

Delilah eventually weaved her way through the traffic and pulled into a parking place. She got out, grabbed her handbag, and locked the car with her keyless remote. A bright smile lit her face. Mari was making her way across the parking lot.

"Hi. Did you just get here, too?"

The two women embraced for a moment. Mari stepped back, rolling her eyes. "I got here about ten minutes before you. With all the after work crowds, it's amazing that we were able to snag parking spaces. Come on. Let's go give reception our names for a table."

Athens, a posh Pasadena restaurant, specialized in Greek

cuisine, and it was tastefully decorated with white pillars, sheer colorful draping, and sanded hardwood floors. The heavy scent of succulent meats and garlic hung in the air. They listed their names for a table before seating themselves on one of the plush white sofas. A table became available soon after as they idly chatted.

The greeter led them to the back of the restaurant, menus in hand. She seated them with a smile and a promise that their server would be with them shortly. Delilah looked around the crowded place for a moment and then turned her attention back to Mari.

"I really needed this tonight. Thanks for meeting up with me."

Mari wrinkled her nose. "Lousy work week?"

She sighed heavily. "Um, not work exactly. This week has been...eventful for other reasons."

Mari grinned, flipping back her long, dark hair. "A new twist in your life? Please dish all about it."

"It's, um, a complicated situation but long story short, because of Declan, I'm involved in a mess with an old family friend."

"How messy on a scale of one to ten?"

"Ten. But, I need this old friend to fix the situation."

Her friend gave her an assessing look. "Male, right?"

Delilah nodded. "Very much an alpha male in every way."

"Hm. Sounds like there could be sparks there."

Delilah looked down for a moment and spoke in a softer voice. "Definitely sparks."

Mari's eyes widened. "Did you and him…?"

She gave her friend a meaningful look. When Mari chuckled and grabbed her hand, heat flushed her cheeks.

"Oh, De! This is exactly the excitement you needed in your life. What's his name?"

"Ash but it's nothing to be excited about. He's there to help me and Declan and that's it. I doubt we'll ever be intimate again."

Mari laughed softly. "Fate may have other plans. You just never know."

———

Later in the evening, they stood side by side dressed in army fatigues at the paint ball range. Delilah adjusted her goggles and quickly took aim at the large target several feet in the distance. She pulled the trigger and fired off shots in rapid succession. She smiled at Mari. "Dead on target. I'm getting better at this."

Her friend grinned and gave a loud whoop. "You've developed some skills in the year we've been coming here. I knew you were a natural. Next year, we move up to a real gun firing range."

She shrugged. "I guess that's a great idea. A year ago, I would've been too afraid to even touch a gun. Paint ball massacre has changed me."

Mari nodded. "Exactly. You live on your own. You really need to know how to protect yourself. We'll start gun shopping in a few weeks if you're up for it."

Delilah's thoughts raced back to the intruder Ash had handled. A gun may not kill a vamp, but it may stop one long enough for her to escape a dangerous situation. "A hand gun sounds like perfect idea."

Mari's gaze moved beyond her. "Antonio and Justin are coming this way. You feel like pairing up for a shoot 'em up in the maze?"

Delilah groaned dramatically. "It would be more fun if Justin would take the hint and stop asking me out."

Mari chuckled. "He's persistent but you've never given him any encouragement."

"Sure. Let's pair up with the guys. I need to work off this aggression."

The thought of Ash and their night together sent a tingle up her spine, even though she was still pissed at his deception. Her eyes narrowed, and she shot off the paint ball gun, focusing on the target which now had Ash's face on it.

Her friend gave her a sly smile. "Maybe you need another round with Ash to take care of that."

49

Ash sat in a chair, across from Queen Galina in the back room of one of the many vamp clubs she owned. She remained silent as she lit a cigarette, a plume of smoke rising. When she was finished with the game of trying to unnerve him, he knew she would finally speak. She took another deep drag, turning her gaze to him.

"Thank you for meeting me here on short notice. We have an important matter to discuss which concerns you."

Ash inclined his head, his face expressionless. "I assume some other vampires in another area require handling."

Galina waved a hand. "Nothing so boring and mundane. This is more of a personal matter."

His jaw clenched at the queen's words. He braced himself for what he was sure would be bad news. "I can't imagine how my personal—"

Galina's voice was sharp. "Every aspect of your life concerns me. You are my servant for the next few decades and, as a result, whatever property you own is subject to seizure and disposal, as the Crown demands. I have your loyalty, yes?"

"My loyalty to the Crown is unquestionable."

Galina's smile was overly cheerful, and Ash had a sinking feeling in the pit of his stomach. "The human woman you've apparently taken up with – this Delilah McDade—she is your property, right?"

He felt the impact of the words like a blow to his chest. His heart hadn't beat in many years, but he swore his pulse raced. He felt a flash of anger the queen didn't even remember Martin McDade, hadn't made the connection between father and daughter. He spoke evenly, maintaining composure. It was in no way a good thing to show the ruthless bitch any trace of emotion or weakness. "Yes, Delilah is my property for the time being. Under the old law, she is indebted to me."

Galina winked. "Then, she is essentially my property. I hate to steal her from your bed, but I need her. As of tonight, I own her, and I have plans for her. She will be sold to an associate of mine at the end of the month. She's to be deeply glamoured, which will make her transition to servant life easier."

Ash spoke through gritted teeth. "Like hell she is. She belongs to me."

Galina subtly cleared her throat. "No, more correctly, she belongs to me. You dare to question my arrangement?"

Ash worked hard to keep his rage tempered, speaking slowly and coldly. "I simply disagree, my Queen."

Her smile was sly. "You're free to disagree but what's done is done. As you are in servitude to the Crown, sometimes sacrifices will be required of you. This is yet another one." She blew smoke into the air, her eyes trained on Ash.

Ash appeared unmoved, but his mind was already spinning with possible ways to get Delilah out this mess he had caused. "Yes, of course," he murmured.

Galina gave him a dismissive wave of her hand. "We'll speak about this matter again soon. In the meantime, feel free to satisfy your lust with one of the many willing vamps out in the club."

Ash stood, heading out of the back room into the main club area. This couldn't happen. He didn't know how he was going to stop it, but he was damned if Galina and her minion associate were even going to get near Delilah. His thoughts turned to his meeting with William Watts later in the evening. There just might be a way to stop this whole thing with his help.

———

Ash traveled the main highway in the hills above Los Angeles, expertly leaning with his motorcycle as the road curved. He had time on his hands before his meeting with William and an evening ride was usually a cure all for his dark moods. He had been troubled by dark thoughts all evening, mainly remembering his maker. His own immortality weighed heavy on him this evening, so he kept riding with no particular destination in mind. He couldn't outrun his problems or his bleak thoughts but the cold wind whipping around made him feel free. An eternity lay out in front of him, but Delilah would be gone in a few, short decades. A part of his humanity remained, reminding him at odd moments how much he envied her and every other human. Immortality was a dark gift, heavy with responsibility and the grave possibility of misery at every turn. His mind flooded with memories of the night he had been forced to surrender his life.

Caddo, California, the past

Ash rubbed the cow's ears, smiling as she happily lowed. He leaned over to speak softly. "Well, Peaches, it's time to go in now that night's coming fast."

The sunset blazed the sky with deep orange and vibrant reds, a few stars already visible as daylight gave way to dusk. Leading Peaches across the grass field, he grinned. He was finally a grown man and free to live as he chose. His parents still lived in town, in his childhood home. He now lived as a cow handler on a small farm in the rural area. It wasn't college, but it was honest work, which pleased his parents, for the time being.

He was halfway to the large barn when he heard the unmistakable deep moaning of an animal in distress. He frowned in confusion. There were only a few cows on the property and he thought Peaches was the last one to lead in. How could he have missed one? Once he had her in her stall, he did a quick head count. Maisie was still out in the field.

Following the sound of distressed moaning, he soon found her down on her back by the fence. It appeared to be a simple task to right her, but he stopped his approach when he realized that her belly was covered in blood. "What the hell—" He moved closer, realizing that her flesh flapped open. Her eyes were wild in panic and pain.

He hightailed it to the foreman's bunker cabin, which was just up the way from his own. The foreman listened intently as he relayed the situation before disappearing from the front door to grab his shotgun. He instructed Ash to quickly head in to his own cabin for the evening, in case they were dealing with a wild wolf or coyote.

"You'll need my help. Let me come with you."

He swore loudly. "No, kid. Do what I told you. I need the more experienced farm hands for this." He quickly brushed passed him.

Ash stood there for a few moments, feeling guilty and helpless. It was his fault a wild animal had gotten to the downed cow. He slowly made his way to his cabin at the end of the row. Once inside, he prepared to settle in for the night. Bathed and dressed for sleeping, he lay stretched out on his small bed, reading a book.

An urgent rap on the door jerked him from his drowsing. Anticipating the foreman, he frowned at the well-dressed man with dark, greying hair standing in front of him. He didn't see too many men in business suits out here in the rural area. The older gentleman smiled, tipping his hat.

"Good evening, son. I'm Gentry. Pleased to make your acquaintance." He extended his hand.

Ash shook it, wearing a small frown. "Pleasure to meet you, Mr. Gentry. I'm not the foreman but how can I help you?"

He waved a hand. "Just Gentry is fine. I'm a traveling merchant who has, unfortunately, run into some trouble. Thieves up there on the main highway have taken my automobile, with everything I own. May I trouble you with a request to rest here with you this evening?"

Ash nodded, ushering him in and taking his coat. "Thieves have become a big problem recently. It's really not safe to travel the highways after the sun sets. Make yourself comfortable and I'll set up a sleeping pallet on the floor for you."

Gentry began a conversation with him as he worked, and he found himself intrigued by the older man's stories of a life lived mainly on the road. He learned about his wife and two children, waiting for his monthly return home to Los Angeles. Ash grew increasingly comfortable in the man's presence, drawn to his boisterous sense of humor. They shared a bottle of whiskey as they talked, seated at the small wood table in the middle of the bunkhouse.

"So, Asher, how long before you allow the pretty girl in your life to settle you down?"

He grinned broadly. "There's no such lady in my life. I figure there's plenty of good years ahead before that happens."

Gentry barked a laugh and the two clinked glasses in a toast. "Amen to that, son. So, there's no one missing you while you work out here on the farm?"

Ash nodded. "Not a soul except my parents, who still live in town."

The older man met his gaze, his tone soft. "Imagine having an eternity of good years ahead and having any woman you wanted – hell, all of 'em." He leaned in closer. "Close your eyes for a moment and consider that idea."

Ash closed his eyes, laughing. "That would be a prayer answered."

Gentry continued speaking gently. "Can you envision it? Never aging, never dying. Picture your hands exploring the soft thighs of some young, vibrant filly who welcomes your touch because she's magically drawn to you. Open your eyes, Asher."

His eyes blinked open and Gentry had moved to stand in front of him, holding his gaze. He forgot what he had been thinking, lost in the intensity of the man's stare. He choked on his words.

Gentry took his face in his hands and Ash tried to move away. "I can give you that gift, son, without the messy business of God being involved. I have that power." He trailed one finger along Ash's neck, smiling. "You really don't have a choice. I haven't had my wife and children around in centuries. They're long dead and buried. I have a different sort of family now and I'm sure you'll fit right in."

Ash was lost in the hypnotic cadence of his words and all he could focus on was the strange glow of the man's eyes. Gentry descended on him and Ash pushed back feebly when the stinging of his neck became monstrous pain. His struggles were weak as his life's blood soaked his night shirt. He realized in horror that the older man was draining his blood with his mouth. His knees buckled, and Gentry caught him in a strong grip.

Gentry laughed softly, blood dripping from lips. "Much better than cow's blood. You're near death now. The only choice you have is me." He ripped open his own wrist with his sharp teeth, lifting it to Ash's parched lips. "Drink me, Asher, and be free."

Ash didn't want to die. He couldn't grasp the unreality of the situation, but he knew what his severe blood loss meant, could feel the effects already. There was no chance of Gentry's blood saving his life but, what if…? Eternal life? A small part of him hesitated before he threw caution to the wind and devoured the blood offered to him with deep gulps.

Gentry ruffled his hair as he drank. "Welcome to my family, kid. Your changeover is happening as I speak. You're about to hurt like hell."

———

Galina sat at the Cherrywood desk in her lavish hotel room, idly drumming her fingers. She had other business to handle in Los Angeles before flying back to Denver. The vampire Romanov, a key business associate, had her irritated at the moment. His return phone call was way overdue, and she was swiftly losing patience. Just as she reached for her cell phone, it chimed. She answered on the first ring.

"Romanov. I've been waiting to hear from you. You're late."

The vamp's voice was smooth. "I'm sorry, my Queen. Other business had me tied up for longer than I anticipated."

"Your first priority is always our business, understood?" Galina snapped. "Now, tell me about our precious cargo. Are the girls glamoured and ready for transport?"

"That's all been handled. They're currently being well guarded in the stock room at your Wilshire District club. As we usually do, we'll have them on a flight to my home in Alaska tonight. The buyers are anxious to inspect and pick up their cargo." He chuckled.

"Excellent. This is welcome news. Are they prepared to fork over the agreed price for each girl?"

"Yes, my Queen. You and I have been at the trafficking game for a long time and I want to be remembered as someone who is good at what he does and never lets you down."

Galina's lips twisted. The old vampire was looking for praise and she tossed him a bone. "I would like to think it will always be this way. You are efficient. The Crown thanks you for you service. Make sure the cargo is on its way tonight and you won't have any problems. Now, about the McDade woman to settle my debt to you. I expect that within a few weeks she can be easily plucked up and ready for you."

Romanov's tone was eager. "Once she's my possession, the debt will be considered settled. She's quite a beauty and I look forward to our first meeting. Lockler needs to be taken down a notch and this is the perfect way."

Jealousy twisted in her gut as she imagined the human woman lying naked with Ash. "Once she's removed, I want her to disappear forever. I want her whereabouts completely untraceable. That's the deal. I'll be in touch." She abruptly ended the call.

She smiled in delight at bringing Ash down a notch for rejecting her subtle invitations to join her back in bed. The idea of his precious McDade woman being used repeatedly for sex and her blood by a dog like Romanov brightened her evening considerably.

———

Like some people could physically sense bad weather coming with achy joints and such, Ash had a gift of sensing trouble, long before it showed up. His nose caught a familiar, musky, unpleasant scent and he wasn't surprised to see Romanov enter the club, flanked by two bodyguards. He was as crafty as he was old and strong. The vamp being in Los Angeles at the same time as Galina usually meant some kind of trouble was brewing.

Ash's instincts screamed at him to stay hidden where he was at a back table. The lighting was dim in that part of the club and it worked to his advantage. Romanov and his crew kept moving quickly towards the rear and they vanished into the spacious back room. He was instantly on his feet, moving in their direction. He stood right outside the closed door, listening intently. His keen hearing picked up on the thread of conversation in progress between Romanov and another male voice, someone who didn't sound familiar.

"Did you glamour them and give them the water bottles?" the old vamp barked. "They still look lucid."

"Yeah. They drank the whole thing. These two will be easy to manage within the hour. The transport vehicle is here."

Ash frowned, his heart dropping with sudden unease. Hearing wasn't good enough. He needed his long-held suspicions about the true nature of Galina and Romanov's business arrangement confirmed with what he could see. He cautiously cracked the door and peered in. The old vampire grabbed a young dark-haired woman by her neck, lifting her up from the chair to her feet. He cursed at her impatiently as she stumbled along to the back door of the place and shoved her into the arms of another vamp.

"That's the both of them. Come on, let's move quickly. There's no time to waste." Romanov and his bodyguards disappeared from his view and the back door slammed abruptly.

Ash's thoughts raced as he played the scene in his head detail by detail. He had his confirmation and he was taking it straight to William and the council. He weaved his way through the throngs of club patrons and was out the heavy glass front doors of the club in seconds flat.

———

"You knew about the trafficking? How long have you and the council known?" Ash, asked, rubbing his hands together in agitation.

William was tall and imposing in his black suit, with a shock of white hair and dark brown skin. Ash had immediately felt comfortable enough to spill his story as they continued their conversation in the back of a plush limousine. He had just spent the better part of twenty minutes explaining his situation to the kindly, older vamp, who now wore a horrified expression.

William nodded. "The council has been investigating Galina for months and only just received confirmation about the trafficking within the last two weeks from various sources, one of whom is Chyna Bentley."

Ash's eyes narrowed. "The vamp who owns the dress boutique in Downtown L.A.? She may prove to be extremely helpful because she hates Galina."

"That is what we've been counting on. Over the past two weeks, we've rescued a small passel of young women, all being funneled through Romanov's compound in Alaska to interested vampire buyers. God only knows how many others have slipped through our fingers."

Ash rubbed his bristled chin, deep in thought. "How were you and the council able to pull off these rescues?"

"Each time we've made it look as if the women were snatched by rival business competitors in an effort to maintain the façade that we, the councilmembers, know very little to nothing of Galina and Romanov's business dealings."

Ash's jaw tensed. "What about the women I saw in the back room of the club tonight?"

William sighed heavily. "We have a team set in place ready to intercept Romanov before he gets to the airport."

"I want in," Ash said flatly. "Tell me where to be and I'll help with the rescue effort."

William shook his head slowly. "It's best that you not get involved at this point. We still need you to be our inside man with Galina."

"Meanwhile, innocent young victims are disappearing without a trace, leaving their families behind to suffer. I can't just do nothing."

"You're doing exactly what we need you to do and it's more than enough. Galina must be stopped and made to pay for her crimes, not just to other vampires but humanity, as well." William paused, his words measured. "I was the only council member who listened to you when you first brought your concerns about her to us long ago."

"No one else seemed to listen."

"Now, due to recent events such as this one, more members are beginning to see her as a threat. Not all, but enough of them see her as a dangerous hindrance to our way of life. We want no harm to humans and wish to live peacefully among them."

Ash nodded. "She's power mad and lives to disrupt everything we have established." He ran a hand through his hair. "The immediate problem is how to extricate Delilah and myself from this situation without risking retaliation and punishment."

William's smile gleamed in the darkness. "A possible solution just came to me. If you're willing to sacrifice your playboy freedom, this will work. Marry her. A wife to a vampire is highly regarded. As your mate, not property, she is untouchable to even the queen. Galina will have no choice but to relent."

Ash turned the proposition over in his mind before speaking. He gave William a smile. "Brilliant thinking, old friend. I need to keep Delilah safe, so I will marry her."

"We can also turn this nightmare mess she created to our advantage. Give the old fox enough rope with this latest scheme and she'll hang herself. Rest assured we want Galina removed from power, her crown empire in shambles. Can we count on you to help us?"

Ash clapped William on the shoulder. "Any and every way I can."

———

As Delilah rounded the corner on the concrete path that lead to her townhouse she saw Ash standing at her doorstep, his gaze focused intently on her. She stopped short for a moment before approaching him slowly.

Her tone was cold and snippy. "I thought you said I would never see you again."

He shrugged. "Your words, not mine." His smile was lethal. "Is that what you really want, Delilah? To never see my face again?"

"Christmas is coming soon. Feel free to gift me that." She pushed past him, trying to ignore her heart thumping as she unlocked her front door. She stepped inside and turned to him. "What in the hell do you want, Ash? You've already satisfied your sexual curiosity about me."

He stepped inside, crowded her back, and closed the door

behind him. "You think my interest in you is purely sexual? You're wrong. I genuinely like you and I can't say that about many humans or vamps. I don't have any regrets about giving you the best sex the other night than you've probably had in a long while. You were free from your inhibitions and that prim exterior."

"I'm the same inside as I am on the outside," she responded tightly. "What you call prim is conservative, logical—"

He shook his head, coming to stand right in front of her. "Controlled and uptight." He reached over and pulled the styling stick from her hair, her long curls falling on her shoulders. Her mouth made a perfect little "O" in surprise at his audacity. "That's better. That's the Delilah I know."

"You don't know me at all! That's the problem. I had sex with a vampire who's just a little too sexually driven for me and it never should've happened. It wouldn't have happened at all if you hadn't intruded into my and Declan's lives."

Ash's expression sobered. "You're right. An intrusion is all I'll ever really bee to you. You're going to hate me before this is over and you're really going to hate what I have to propose to you."

She raised her chin. "What is it that you have to propose to me that I'm almost certain I will hate?"

"It's a real proposal. You have to marry me, Delilah. You and your brother's safety depend on it."

FIVE

She let out a shocked gasp. "Are you insane? Marry you?"

He nodded. "It's the only way I can protect you."

"Protect me from who?" she scoffed.

"I answer to my queen and, to punish me, she's targeted you to be a servant to another vamp. You wouldn't be anything to him but a blood bag that he fucks."

Delilah closed her eyes for a moment, taking in everything. Her head was spinning. She spoke softly. "Why is marrying me necessary? I'm sorry. I don't understand vamp politics at all."

He caressed her cheek for a moment. "As my wife, only I would have claim to you. You would be regarded very highly, even though you're not a vamp. Galina, the queen, would have no rights to claim you as she would my property." He heaved a deep sigh. "Damn it. I've brought you nothing but trouble since day one. By vampire law, when I paid off the debt, you became my property, and I'm sorry for that."

She licked her lips, swallowing nervously. "Will...will they come after Declan if I don't marry you?"

"Almost certainly. Wearing my ring is the only protection you'll have. Galina is ruthless and, in doing this, I'll surely incur her wrath, but she'll be powerless in this situation. I've never married so this will take her by surprise, which works in our favor. Say yes and we'll be on a flight tonight to Vegas for a quiet ceremony and Declan will be on a flight to one of my properties in Seattle. I picked it because it's in a quiet, private community where he can't cause any more trouble." His eyes narrowed. "Say no and I'll have to glamour you again until after the ceremony."

Her eyes widened. "That's no kind of choice! The last thing I want is to be your wife but you're holding Declan's safety over my head and threatening to wipe my mind clean again, all in the name of protection. Are there no other options? What if we went on an extended vacation overseas?"

Ash snorted. "Galina is like a relentless bloodhound. She would find you wherever you ran off to. This is the only option, trust me."

Delilah's shoulders slumped, and it took all of her effort to stand there, searching his face. She hardened her expression. "Marrying me, even for our protection, is going to cost you big. I have a career that I love, and I can't just take six months off to jet around the world like a rich woman, which I'm not. The most time I can take off right now is two weeks. Added to my holiday time off, that's three weeks we have to get us out of this mess. It's definitely time for Declan to return to college, but I'm not paying for it anymore. You are."

She poked hard at his chest. "I want a full financial ride for Declan's college education. I also want a big settlement since I have to surrender my single status for quite some time. There are many potential, educated, and wealthy suitors I'll be missing out on meeting so a large, neat parcel of cash and a property you own should well compensate me. We won't be consummating this marriage, so an annulment should be easy. I'm sure, with your underworld connections, it'll be even easier. All I asked for or no deal."

Ash's lips curved in a half-smile. "Deal, you little extortionist."

She raised an eyebrow. "Not an extortionist. I'm simply being pragmatic."

"There's a catch and here comes the best part. Vampire marital unions are forever and binding, Delilah."

"You mean I can't divorce you? Ever?"

"No, you'll always be regarded as my wife in the vamp community, if not legally. Relax. I won't hold you to your vows." His tone was amused. "We can't ever divorce but we can live separate lives. Once the heat's off, you and I will go our separate ways and I'll grant you a human legal divorce so that you can marry some nice, educated, boring human guy."

"You're trying not to laugh and it's pissing me off. Fine, whatever. Let's just get married as soon as possible."

Ash nodded, reaching into his back pocket for his wallet. He handed her a black credit card. "We'll go to Vegas for the ceremony tonight and fly back home soon after. Tell your family, friends, and your job whatever you need to."

Delilah murmured, already lost in her thoughts. "There's just Declan and me. Both of our parents have passed on and we don't really know any of our other family members."

"You'll need some new flashy clothes as well as a wedding dress. Go nuts with the credit card. I can easily handle the expense. Also, when this is over, you'll get a generous separation settlement from me. It's only fair given what I've put you through."

He strode to the front door. "I'll send a car for you at midnight that will take you to the airport where I'll be waiting." He gave her a parting look as he left, closing the door behind him.

Delilah breathed in deeply. Her mind had difficulty processing her current situation. She was marrying a vamp she barely knew. *You know him enough to know he'll keep you safe.* Every day she felt her anger at him melting a little more.

She grabbed up her purse and headed for the door. She had only a few hours to get her shopping done and get ready. As she locked her door, she heard the roar of a motorcycle. She came around the corner in enough time to see Ash in his leather jacket and helmet fly away from the curb. She was learning new things about him every time they talked, and she honestly couldn't say that she didn't like it.

———

"See, didn't I tell you my skills as a wedding planner would come in handy for you, someday," Mari said.

Delilah gave her a small smile. "I just never thought so soon and under these circumstances."

The two were in an upscale lingerie boutique on trendy Green Street. She stroked a crimson satin lingerie teddy displayed on a table, feeling like a fraud. The romantically dim lighting and the expensive vintage furniture all screamed that this was an experience meant for women in love.

"Maybe we can skip this part. It's not like I'll be displaying any of this stuff for Ash anytime soon."

Mari gave her a wicked smile. "Oh, honey, these little scraps of lace and satin are more for you to enjoy. Besides, Ash can easily afford this. When I saw that little black credit card he gave you, I knew he meant serious business. He's loaded and he's marrying you to help you and Declan. I'd wrap him up and take him home. Enough said."

Delilah's heart lightened at the thought that she and Declan were now well protected. Her lips curved. "Well, maybe just a few things," she murmured.

Mari chuckled. "Atta girl. We have your wedding dress and heels. Now, we need a few things that may tempt Ash to consider this marriage as more than a business arrangement." At Delilah's groan, she rolled her eyes. "You just never know."

Later, Delilah was home from her last-minute shopping trip with Mari for a few minutes when she heard a key grate in the front door lock. Only one other person had access to her home, so she wasn't surprised to see Declan poke his head inside before coming in and closing the door behind him. She instantly felt a knot of tension form in her stomach as she embraced him. He held her tightly in a bear hug for long, silent moments, before stepping back to look into her eyes.

"De, what have I involved us in? Ash Lockler called me and he said exactly two things. Pack my heavy winter stuff because I was going on a trip he's paying for and ask my sister to explain why before I left. He sent a car to pick me up twenty minutes later. What the hell is going on here?"

She cleared her throat. "This is all about keeping us safe. I won't go into too many details, but Ash has decided that L.A. isn't safe for us right now so he's, um, handling the situation."

He swore under his breath, his hands trembling. "I thought the heat was off now that my debt was paid. Ash assured me."

"It goes deeper than that, unfortunately but you even becoming involved in the underworld was a dangerous move."

"What does this have to do with you?"

She embraced him, kissing his forehead lightly. She found it hard to meet his gaze. "Everything I'm doing is to protect you and to secure your future."

Declan shook his head vehemently. "I really hate the sound of that. What exactly are you doing and how does it involve Ash Lockler?"

"I'm marrying him tonight in Las Vegas while you'll be safely on a private flight to Seattle, where you won't cause me any more grief. You don't need to know much more than that."

"What the—are you nuts?"

She shook her head slowly, her expression calm, as if she hadn't just stated the craziest thing ever. Her words were measured. "My thinking is just fine. Trust me, this is the only way out of this mess. Even though you've made some really poor decisions in the past year, I'm not totally blaming you, but when you tried to use me to pay your debt, and he paid it instead, it made me his property. Some kind of vampire law. Now his queen wants to claim me. Marrying him is the only way to stop her. Once this is over, Ash will go his way and we'll go ours. No more underworld connections. Ever. You return to that life, I'm cutting you off. Got it?"

He fidgeted for a moment, nodding. "Yeah, I got it. I don't know much about him, but I know he's good at what he does so I'm sure you'll be safe while you're with him."

"I trust him enough and stop acting like I'm some ignorant, small village maiden who can't take care of herself." She pushed him towards the front door. "Go. Don't keep your driver waiting. You need to be in Seattle as soon as possible."

While the two hugged each other tightly, Declan kissed her cheek. "Call my cell the minute you touch down in Vegas."

She nodded as he waved before he headed down the concrete path. He disappeared around the corner and tears sprang to her eyes. She hated the thought of being separated from her brother, even for a few weeks. She'd been right there for every skinned knee, every bedtime story, every angry moment he'd had without a father.

She pinched her lips together. This wasn't just about her. It was about Declan and she would do whatever she had to do to protect him.

———

Delilah settled herself into the plush, crème leather seat, leaning back with her eyes closed. They were aboard Ash's private jet, speeding towards Las Vegas. She mentally calculated they were about a half hour away from their destination and feigning exhaustion was the best way to avoid talking to him. She would be married to him very soon but that didn't mean she had to share her tangled, confused thoughts with him. He sat across from her, his legs occasionally brushing hers.

"You can't seem to keep your eyes closed and I have the strangest feeling you don't want to talk to me."

"I don't." Her eyes remained closed.

"We're doing this to keep you and your brother safe. No hidden agenda or ulterior motives. I can't marry anyone but you in my lifetime so, believe me, I'm not particularly thrilled to walk down the aisle, either. You're my responsibility now and I will look out for you."

Her eyes snapped open at the gentleness of his tone. She relented, suddenly feeling like an ungrateful bitch. "Yes, I know you will. Look, I'm sorry to give you such a hassle constantly. You didn't force me into anything. I agreed to this so let's move forward and make the best of it." She extended her hand. "Friends from here on out?"

He shook her hand and held it for a long moment. "Friends."

Curiosity got the better of her. "How did a simple country boy from Northern California come to build an immense underworld empire?"

He shrugged. "Thanks to my mother I've always been good with finances. I've been around for over a hundred years. Given that amount of time, I imagine anyone with business savvy can do what I've done."

She cleared her throat, suddenly nervous as she realized they weren't arguing for the first time since her memory returned. They were holding a conversation and she wanted to know more about him. "You said that you work for your queen. Are you her accountant?"

Ash's chuckle warmed her heart a little. "Hell, no. My work for Galina has nothing to do with numbers unless it's about her money disappearing. I'm her enforcer, honey."

"You mean—you shoot people? You're an enforcer like the one who killed my dad?"

"Rarely anyone human. We're forbidden to hurt or kill humans without just cause, regardless of Galina's demands. I only kill vampires and human trash when there's a need for it."

Her eyes narrowed thoughtfully. "I assume you're armed now."

He flipped back his suit jacket, exposing his sheathed gun. His fangs extended for a brief moment before he retracted them. "Armed in the best ways possible." He gave her a thorough once over. "You look angelic in your wedding dress with your curls hanging loose and that touch of baby's breath."

Her heart beat a little faster. "Thank you. I, um, hired my best friend, Mari, at the last minute to help me shop and prepare."

His tone was gently teasing. "Did she help you pick out lingerie for the wedding night?"

She recognized that he was only poking fun and relaxed, smiling. "Yes, but you'll never see it."

"Little Ms. Prim," he murmured.

———

A comfortable silence settled between them as Delilah focused her attention outside the small window. She leaned her head back and, gradually, her eyelids drooped. Ash knew by her deep even breaths that she was asleep. He tossed back another shot of whiskey, his thoughts taking a dark turn to the past. He remembered another bride on her wedding day.

Denver, Colorado, the past

*Ash followed the concrete path in the rose garden behind the large cathedral. His senses were heightened from the adrenaline that rushed through him and from an exorbitant amount of whiskey shots. His anger exploded as he spotted Galina off to the side of the path, **her** fingertips stroking the rose petals. By now, he knew this was a game to her. She had passed by his table in the banquet hall, giving him a meaningful look as she headed out the doors to the garden. He was expected to follow, and he cursed himself for doing just that.*

"Mrs. Saburova," he addressed her coldly as he approached. "You needed something?"

She looked up, her gaze direct. "Yes, Ash, I need you."

He kept his eyes level, snipping off each word. "I'm sure the only one you need now is your new husband Dmitri, my Queen."

Galina moved towards him and he stepped back. She shook her head slowly. "I told you nothing between you and I has changed. Marrying Dimitri was good business and nothing more." Ignoring the thorns, she casually plucked a rose. "It's you I want in my life and in my bed."

Ash snorted. "But again, no mention of love. I'm good for a fuck whenever you need it, but I can't be by your side in the moments that really count for something." He rubbed his eyes. "I'm done, Galina – with you, with all of this. I'm here to serve the Crown until my sentence is over and not a damn thing else."

Her eyes glimmered with suppressed violence and she crumpled the rose. She lifted her hand, now dripping with blood from the thorns. "It feels just like this to lose you." She quickly moved past him and back down the path towards the cathedral.

Ash watched her go, surprised by his satisfaction at seeing her pain. Loving her had already cost him so much. He knew it would be hard to break her sexual hold on him, but he'd made his decision. A big part of him was relieved to be free of the weight of Galena's obsessive kind of love. He slowly made his way back down the path and resolved to keep drinking until his own pain went away.

———

Watching Delilah sleep, Ash contemplated their situation. Tonight, like Galina, he would also marry for a business arrangement. He chuckled to himself at the irony. His only saving grace was he was doing this to protect Delilah and her brother. The problem was he wasn't sure whether that made him a bastard for dragging them deeper into his dangerous, complicated world or a savior.

———

Delilah checked her reflection in the long mirror in the back of the chapel. She and Ash were far from the hustle of the main strip. It was quiet in this part of the desert city and the air was chilly. She looked and felt beautiful in the white fitted, strapless lace dress that fell to her knees. She had even found vibrant, silver three-inch heels that complimented the dress perfectly. She fluffed her hair a bit after applying a second coat of light plum lip gloss. The music queued up and her knees wobbled a bit as she grabbed her small rose and baby's breath bouquet from the small dressing table. She opened the door and walked down the long hallway to the main part of the chapel. The pastor stood at the altar, holding his Bible with a welcoming smile. Her gaze shifted to Ash standing there, strikingly handsome in his dark suit with his blond hair neatly combed.

The part of her that wanted to survive this overrode the part of her that wanted to run, and her lips curved in a smile, walking down the aisle to her new life. Every moment after she reached the altar and stood across from Ash passed as a blur. She murmured her vows, her eyes trained on his face. He softly spoke the words that would bind them as husband and wife before—at the pastor's urging—he'd seared her soul with a kiss that was far from the chaste peck she had expected. Tingles radiated in her core and she hastily looked away from the heat in Ash's eyes.

———

The bed was awfully small. Delilah turned the sleeping arrangements over in her mind, wondering how on earth she could sleep comfortably lying so close to him if he insisted on sharing the bed. It occurred to her suddenly that Ash probably never slept in a bed, probably in a safe casket somewhere else. He had explained to her that sunlight didn't kill vamps but considerably weakened them.

She looked around the bedroom of the suite in one of the more upscale hotels in Vegas. The room was done in tasteful shades of gold and black. The view from the twenty floors up was breathtaking with the entire city laid out for miles. Ash had gone to feed, leaving her alone in the hotel room with an armed guard right outside the door.

She replayed the brief wedding ceremony in her mind. Some parts were a blur but others, like she and Ash speaking their vows and his warm, rough kiss that left her trembling a little, stayed with her. It hadn't been the wedding of her dreams, with her walking down the aisle to a man she loved, but still it had her thinking that Ash was as good as his word. She needed protection and he had provided it, with zero strings attached. Her anger had faded into a calm acceptance of the way things were. Having sex with him had been a more than pleasurable experience but something to never be repeated. No need to overthink it.

Delilah closed her silk robe tightly as Ash entered the hotel room, calling her name. He rapped on the bedroom door. "Are you decent?"

"Yes, I'll be right out."

"Good, because I got you a little something."

She hastily opened the door to find him standing at the table. He held a small, decorated Christmas tree in one hand. He smiled, beckoning her to come closer. She felt her heart catch at his thoughtfulness and moved closer to touch the ornamented branches.

"This tree is meant as an apology for wrecking your holiday celebration with your friends and loved ones. I wanted you to feel festive while we're here. I noticed you don't have a tree in your home yet." He set the tree down on the table.

"It's really lovely, Ash. Thank you." Her eyes welled up with tears and she lowered her head.

He caught one falling teardrop with his thumb. "Why the tears?"

"This is my first Christmas without Declan and he's the only family I have." She waved her hand. "I'm just being overly sentimental."

Ash guided her over to the sofa and pulled her into his arms. They sat that way for a few, silent moments before he spoke. "I have no one in this world who cares about me, so I understand your feelings of abandonment better than anyone else you'll ever meet. There's no shame in crying about the loneliness. I've been waiting decades to feel better but that feeling never comes. You're not totally alone, Delilah. You have your brother and friends who care about you. I care about you, not that it means much."

She rested her head on his shoulder and gave into the tears for long moments. She sniffled, taking a deep, calming breath. "The loneliness gets overwhelming at times. Yes, I have a good life but I'm missing a family life and, every year the holidays end this way." She gave him a bleary smile. "Except this year, I'm crying all over my new husband."

"Which I don't mind at all."

"Thank you for caring about me." She stroked his face with soft fingertips and didn't pull away when he settled his lips on hers in gentle kiss.

He kissed her forehead, moving her from his lap to the sofa. "I wouldn't dare try to share a bed with you so this is where I'll sleep. Even with the blinds drawn, I'll be weak during the day, but I don't dare go to ground to rest and leave you unprotected. You're safe with me, Delilah. Trust me. I'm not a threat." He stood up abruptly. "You'll have an armed guard with you at all times, but I still don't think it's safe for you to be without me while we're here. Please stay in the rooms and lay low during the day while I'm sleeping. We'll go out to the casinos on the strip tonight, if you like."

She nodded, before she turned and walked slowly to the bedroom. She managed another little smile. "I would like that." She stood in the doorway. "Good night, Ash."

"Good night, Mrs. Lockler."

She closed the door, leaning back against it. Hearing her new last name made it all so final, but it was far from the hellish experience she had expected. She twisted the heavy gold wedding band on her finger, remembering slipping the matching one on Ash's finger. He wore her ring but that didn't mean he truly belonged to her by any stretch, no matter how sweet and caring he was to her. That was something she couldn't afford to let herself forget. She grabbed her cell phone from her handbag, intent on calling Declan.

Later, after assuring her brother that she was safe in Vegas with Ash, she stretched out on the plush bed. The warm air coming through the vents above her had her drowsing off. Her mind wandered to an old memory.

Pasadena, California – The Past

"Keep stirring that cake batter, honey. No lumps means it's ready."

Delilah grinned at her grandma, whipping the spoon around in the big bowl. "I'm thirteen this year, Maw Maw, and that means I know how to make a cake."

They stood across from each other in the spacious kitchen, the afternoon sun filtering in through the half-closed window blinds. They both were decoratively festive in their matching aprons. Baking with her grandma during the winter holidays was a tradition, with her earning more responsibility with each treat they made together.

Maw Maw leaned over to peek into the bowl and grinned. "Excellent job, kiddie." They high-fived each other. "It's time for me to take over. Yes, you're thirteen now, which means soon you'll be into boys and makeup with no time to cook with me."

Delilah rolled her eyes. "For every cute boy I like at my school, there's ten I don't. I'll never give up cooking with you to hang out with immature cretins like that. Besides, I still have my heart set on my very own vampire, like you had, Maw Maw." She gave her a sassy smile and drew her finger along the top of the bowl for batter to lick.

"Oh, honey bear." Maw Maw waved a careless hand. "That was my life in the south ages ago. I didn't realize my little stories of hanging out with the vampires in my youth would make such an impression on you. What's wrong with human boys?"

Delilah wrinkled her nose in disdain. "Boring! I want a vampire like the one who walked thirty miles to your house in a rain storm to bring you a sweet gift."

Maw Maw laughed. "Be careful what you ask the heavens for, my girl. You may just end up with your own vampire and have no idea what to do with him." She turned back to the counter. "Now, let's get those cake pans ready."

Delilah came back to the moment wearing a sleepy smile. Her grandmother would be tickled if she could see her married to a vampire who was anything but boring. She rolled over, drifting off.

———

Ash waited until the well after the light went off in Delilah's room before he grabbed his cell phone. He was relieved when William answered on the first ring. "Any news?"

"The council has arranged the binding ceremony for you and Delilah when you return from your honeymoon. Galina will have to be present, which will put her in Los Angeles where she may meet up with Romanov. As her enforcer, you're in a unique position to keep us supplied with intel. We need you to be our eyes and ears."

"My thoughts exactly," Ash said. "Delilah and her brother are safe which means I can shift my focus to Galina and Romanov."

"Very good. Enjoy your time with your new wife and I'll be in touch."

"Thanks, William." He ended the call and placed his phone on the small table. He was already thinking of ways to gather more incriminating evidence against Galina and Romanov. It occurred to him that with his small, private security team, he had eyes and ears of his own. For decades, the queen had been untouchable, and he needed every advantage at his disposal to help take her down.

———

"You look stunning in that next to nothing dress," Ash whispered in Delilah's ear as she pulled the lever of the casino slot machine.

"You're attracting far too much attention for me to feel comfortable."

Her full lips curved in a smile as she looked away from the bright screen to meet his eyes. She had picked up a sexy snug dress in royal blue with matching high heels in one of the shops earlier that afternoon. His armed guard had escorted her to one of the most exclusive boutiques in Vegas after she had begged Ash incessantly to allow it.

"Hmm...thank you. Now, aren't you glad you let me go shopping?" Delilah pulled the slot lever again and groaned as it ate another quarter. She sipped from her glass of champagne. They had been in one the private VIP rooms of the casino for the past two hours and she had been losing far more money than she won. She hadn't been in a casino in a few years and declined Declan's invitations because she saw no fun in losing precious, hard earned money. Tonight, she was actually having fun, but she was almost sure it was because she was with Ash.

He placed his arms on either side of her and grabbed the lever with one hand. He pushed the denominator button on the slot machine, changing it from playing quarters to playing five dollars a bet. He spoke right next to her ear. "You're getting nowhere because you keep playing it safe with the small bets. You're loaded now, honey, with enough money to set you for life. You need to gamble like it."

Keeping his hand on hers, he pulled the lever down and they both watched the machine flash brightly and spin. When she won twenty dollars, she laughed in pleased surprise. The third time they pulled the lever together, the screen lit up with a multitude of bright colors and the siren on the top of the slot machine blared loudly. She watched in amazement as the winning amount showed on the screen. She looked at Ash to see his lips turned in an amused smile.

"You hit the minor jackpot. Congrats."

"Did I really just win two thousand dollars?"

He nodded. "That's drinking fun money for us. Just for

enduring the pleasure of my companionship as my wife for a few months, you're worth so much more than that." He sipped champagne, keeping his eyes on her. "You ready to head back to the hotel?"

She nodded, her eyes bright and her cheeks flushed from the alcohol and the excitement.

As they approached the cashier's counter to turn in their winning tickets, she watched him pull a few hundred dollar bills from his wallet and toss them on the counter. The attendant, a young blond man in a red vest, smiled in greeting.

"Please take whatever the tickets are worth plus these bills and donate them to one of the children's funds." Ash's voice was low.

Delilah blinked in surprise, fiddling with the tickets she held. Her heart was full to see the kind, giving part of him again. She stopped the attendant as he moved away "Wait. Take half of my winning tickets and please do the same. The rest I would like in big bills." She faced Ash, intensely intrigued. "I never imagined you would be so gracious and thoughtful with your money." She sighed. "Seeing as you gave me an unexpected windfall on the slot machine, I wish I could give all my money away, too, but there's always Declan to consider."

They collected their money and Ash put a guiding hand on the small of her back as they headed for the casino's black frosted front doors. His jaw was tense. "Your brother is now my financial responsibility as long as we're legally married. I hate him taking advantage of you. Your brother needs to grow up."

She shrugged as they stepped outside into the chilly night air, grateful when he wrapped her in his black suit jacket. She clutched her tiny purse tightly. "He has only me left in this life."

Their limousine rounded the large circular driveway and Ash helped her inside. She sat across from him, noting his eyes on her as they pulled away into traffic. She bit her bottom lip nervously and his eyes followed the movement. "I was wrong to judge you so harshly, Ash. You're a good man deep down where it counts. I never expected you to be concerned about children's welfare or me and my brother."

He loosened his tie, looking away from her. "So, we're beyond all that mess at the vamp club and then later at your home?"

Delilah's head was swimming from the alcohol, but she could still give him an answer. "What you did at the club was meant to protect me, though I wish you had been more honest and upfront with me." She inched closer. She cupped his face in her hands. "The night we, um, had sex was something I wanted very much. I enjoyed it."

"Your eyes are very big and I'm sure you're buzzed from the champagne. While I appreciate you telling me I'm one of your favorite people, tomorrow we'll be back to arguing again." The corner of his lip turned up as he stroked her forehead. "Or you'll just freeze me out completely."

"You brought me a little Christmas tree." She smiled, sure that her face was as loopy as she felt but she didn't care. She rested one hand on his thigh.

"Delilah, don't go looking for trouble. I care about your well-being but right now, you're making it hard for me to leave it at that." He gently moved her hand away. She put it back. He sighed deeply. "Are you offering yourself to me?"

She tilted her head, giving him a smoldering look of desire before she kissed the corner of his mouth. "Uhm-hmm. I'm curious what it would be like to feel you on top of me again, pushing deeply inside—"

Ash grabbed her arms, jerked her to him. "Oh, fuck this." He lowered his mouth onto hers, parting her lips with his tongue. He tasted of champagne and hot, heady passion. She savored every moment of his lips traveling the length of her neck. He murmured against her throat. "If you don't stop me, the first thing I'm going to do when we get back to the hotel is devour every inch of you."

He nibbled her earlobe and she moaned as his hands cupped her breasts.

"Why would I stop you?"

He stretched her out beneath him, his weight heavy on her. His mouth plundered hers as his hands caressed her thighs, slowly moving upwards. Her panties dampened as he stroked her through the blue lace. The limo came to a stop outside their hotel and Ash moved away, straightening the bottom of her dress.

"Inside, honey. Now." His voice was rough with need.

He grasped her hand tightly and helped her out of the car before near dragging her to one of the elevators. The moment the door closed, she launched herself at him, kissing his face until they reached their floor. He grabbed her around the waist and pulled her out and down the hallway. He used the key card, pushed open the door, moved her inside, and slammed it shut.

Ash stood completely still in front of her. He lifted her chin. "Is this a game to you? Are you completely unaware of what you do to me? Please don't change your mind in the middle of me loving you. This attraction—I'm not used to being this much on fire for a woman and I'm not sure yet if I like it." His jaw tensed.

Delilah softened her voice. "This is all new to me, too. I like you and I like the way you make me feel. You showed me the way lovemaking should be." She moved the hair from his face. "Tonight, I'm relaxed and happy. I want to give myself to you. It doesn't have to go beyond this. You have a life to return to when our marriage is over and so do I. I want as many good memories from this experience as I can possibly get."

He cocked an eyebrow. "This is the real you under that Ms. Prim exterior." He took her hand and led her to the bedroom.

SIX

In his wildest dreams, Ash had never expected to see this side of Delilah again. He vowed to himself to be gentle and slow with her this time around, but his cock was hard, and he couldn't think beyond the moment. He closed the door, pulling her to him. Planting soft kisses on the tops of her breasts, he slid the straps down. He helped her shimmy out of her dress and pulled the heels from her feet. She stood before him in her blue lace bra and panties. The moonlight coming in from the large window glinted off her beautiful light brown skin and the glorious curls framing her face and draped over her shoulders.

"Come here, honey."

She came to stand in front of him and he turned her around. He unclipped her bra and tossed it to the floor. He embraced her from behind and cupped her full breasts in his hands. His fingers lowered to trace her belly before moving up again to play with her hardened nipples. She gasped, and he continued his gentle assault, satisfied that she was on fire from him. He slid his fingers into her panties, pleased to find her wet and welcoming. Teasing her, he nipped the nape of her neck with his fangs. She leaned back against his chest as he found her sensitive bud and toyed with it. He released her and pushed her back onto the bed.

He stripped down quickly as she watched him with sensually narrowed eyes. When he was bare, she stretched out her arms to embrace him. He lay beside her and caressed her body from neck to navel. Moving on top of her, he kissed his way across her belly and thighs. He tugged at the tiny panties, pulling them off. His tongue slid into her core, darting in and out. Her hand rested on the top of his head as she loudly moaned her pleasure when his tongue flicked her bud repeatedly. He looked up at her face. "I don't want you to come just yet."

She surprised him when she sat up and straddled him. She ran her tongue across his hard chest and downward, following the line of his abs until she reached his stiff cock. She grasped him in one hand, circling the tip with light fingers until he growled low in his throat. He felt like he needed air, gasping. He cursed loudly when her tongue replaced her fingertips in a playful swirl around the tip. He realized in a split second that Delilah was all take no prisoners when she was turned on. He felt as if he was losing control of the situation fast.

She looked up at him, removing her mouth. Her voice was a whisper. "I want you inside me when you come."

He grabbed her and reversed their positions. He moved between her legs, putting himself at her entrance. She wrapped her shapely legs up around his waist and cried out as he slid himself inside of her. His thrusts were slow and gentle for long moments before speeding up a little as her hips moved. She was all wet softness and he felt her yield to accommodate him as he went even deeper. He pinned her arms above her head and kissed her intensely. "You're so soft everywhere. Your beautiful skin, your hair —touched by moonlight."

He kept a steady pace of movement, rocking his hips in ways he knew would bring her the greatest pleasure. She ran her nails down his back, digging in, and even the slight sting of it made him hotter. He could tell she was on the edge by the slight hitch in her breathing and he smiled to himself when she had her orgasm seconds later, calling out his name. He continued thrusting for long moments until he came hard, his eyes closing tightly at the rush of sensation.

Ash pulled her into arms, resting his chin on her head. He felt her body tremoring and stroked her hair softly to calm her in the darkness.

———

Delilah's eyes flickered open, the sunlight coming in the window of the hotel room hurting her eyes. She sat up, Ash's absence bringing a twinge of disappointment. She caught sight of a white hotel stationary envelope with her name on it and rose from the bed, wrapping herself in a sheet. *It's a bit late for modesty.* Her lips curved in a secretive smile. Ash may not be a real husband, but he was most definitely her lover. She surprised herself with the calm acceptance that she was falling for him and she wanted him in her life, and in her bed, for as long as he was willing to be there.

His note told her that she was to remain in the hotel room for the day as he rested elsewhere, and he would send a car for her later that evening to take her to the airport. They would be flying back to Los Angeles. He was brief, none of his words hinting at his feelings about their night together, not that she had expected him to. She was coming to know him better than he would probably like, and she knew he prided himself on emotional control. The fact that she could make him lose it, even a little bit, pleased her as she gathered her things together to hop in the shower. He had been gentle and passionate in his loving with her last night. Her heart yearned to see that part of him far more often.

———

Galina dropped her cell phone on the bed and let out a stream of loud curse words. Married. Ash was married to that simpering human idiot. She kicked an expensive wood chair across her bedroom. She was expected to give her blessing at the union ceremony, in front of the elders and a crowd of other vamps. She dug her fingernails into her hand. She was furious at Ash's strategic move and vowed to herself to win this battle between them. It was almost time for his wife to disappear forever, thanks to Romanov.

She dialed the vamp's number and had him on the line within seconds. "I'm sure you've heard about Lockler's marriage to the human bitch."

"Yes, I have. Does this mean she won't be delivered to me as promised?" Romanov's voice was smooth.

Galina was careful to keep the rage and panic out of her voice. "On the contrary, she will be delivered to you earlier. Lockler believes his wife is safe from me now, with the blessing of the council. It's best to let him think that way. He will be completely blindsided when she disappears."

Romanov chuckled. "One of your best strategies, my Queen."

"What about the new batch of girls? Are they ready for transport the night of the union ceremony in Los Angeles?"

Romanov's voice was eager. "Yeah, everything is arranged. Now, about the McDade woman. When—"

Galina abruptly cut him off. "I will keep you informed, as needed. Make sure there are no screw ups with the transport." She ended the call.

She desperately wanted things between her and Ash to go back to the way they once were. The only thing standing between her and her happiness with him was about to vanish. Her lips twisted in a little smile.

———

"Ash, do we really have to do this whole wedding celebration thing tomorrow night?" Delilah's nose wrinkled delicately. She sat across from him as they made the distance from Las Vegas back to Los Angeles. "I'm uncomfortable meeting all these underworld associates of yours, especially your queen. Not only did she have my dad killed, she tried to sell me." She tried to keep her voice light with humor, but it cracked with emotion.

His smile was crooked. "I'm not thrilled about it but it's no good to break tradition. The Council of Elders and Queen Galina must bless our union. I think it'll be fun to watch her squirm because you're untouchable as my wife. Don't worry. I'll be next to you the whole time."

"I worry about your idea of fun."

He pierced her with a look, his voice slightly rough. "What about last night? Was that fun?"

Her heart raced as she gave him a level look, heat shooting up her neck and blooming in her cheeks. "It was every bit as fun as I imagined it would be."

He let out a bark of laugh, lacing his fingers with hers. "You surprise me in the most intriguing ways."

Delilah delicately sucked on his fingertip, boldly meeting his gaze. Ash drew in a deep breath and her pussy ached in response.

"Don't start with me unless you aim to finish," he said softly.

She crawled into his lap with a wicked smile. She planted tiny kisses all over his face as his arms banded around her. "Finishing with you is exactly what I'm aiming for," she whispered in his ear.

Ash lifted her into position right on his cock and she began to slowly grind against him. He parted her lips with a searing kiss, his tongue playing with hers. His hands slid beneath her black dress and caressed her smooth thighs, inciting her to go beneath his T-shirt and play with his male nipples. She nibbled his ear and he groaned as her hands drifted lower. She deftly unzipped his jeans and cradled his hard cock in her hands, gently stroking the tip.

He lifted her up for a moment and grasped the crotch of her tiny panties, moving them aside. Soft lips left hers to travel down her neck to the tops of her breasts and she sighed in passion. He pushed the top of her dress down to get to her hardened nipples with his tongue. Playing with her, he caught every gasp from her parted lips with his own. Her breaths came out in a hiss as he found her bud and played with it.

Delilah leaned back to look at him and was pleased to see his eyes narrowed in desire for her. "Please, no more torture, Ash. I want you inside me."

He removed his fingers from her and she lifted up a bit to guide him into her soft pussy. She cried out and his mouth claimed hers again as he filled her completely. She ground down on him, wrapping her arms around his broad shoulders as she met his thrusts. She felt wanton, miles above the earth with an alpha vamp deep inside her.

With his hand down between them, he toyed with her bud as he moved inside her. Her body exploded in deep pleasure and a moment later he climaxed, shaking in her arms. She was a trembling mess, feeling weightless after the onslaught of his loving. He cradled her as she rested her head on his chest.

"I've never been loved as thoroughly as I have with you. Sex was always just a meaningless act for me, with the wrong guys. Being with you has changed all that. You make it beautiful."

Ash tilted her chin up and kissed her softly. "You're beautiful, Delilah, and far too precious for casual sex. I care about you deeply, probably more than I should. You need to know this is more than casual, even after we go our separate ways."

Delilah held him even tighter, tears forming in her eyes. One day soon this would all be over and all she would have was memories. She kissed his cheek. "Thank you, Ash," she whispered.

The pilot's voice boomed from the cockpit, announcing that they were a few minutes away from landing and they hastily fixed their clothes. They belted themselves in their seats, with Ash sitting across from her. Delilah looked out the window at the beautiful view of Los Angeles lit up at night. Ash gestured at her and she lifted her legs into his lap. He slid off her heels and gently rubbed her feet. She smiled and leaned her head back against the seat, closing her eyes.

————

"Oh, you're radiantly beautiful," Mari gushed as she tightly cinched the corset back of Delilah's black full-length gown.

She met her friend's eyes in the mirror and smiled. "Are you sure I'm not wearing too much makeup?"

"No, it looks fine."

"I'm wearing my natural curls tonight. Should I maybe do a nice bun? Would I look more elegant?"

Mari shook her head. "You are the epitome of elegance already, with a touch of delicious that Ash will appreciate. Your intimate little wedding must have been beautiful." She stepped back, letting Delilah admire herself in the mirror.

Delilah nodded. "It was everything I ever dreamed about," she admitted. She had imagined the ceremony would be rushed and awkward, but instead she'd felt cherished by Ash.

Her friend chuckled. "I can't wait to meet Ash tonight. What time is he coming for you?"

"He should be here in about ten minutes. I'm so nervous and jittery about the event tonight."

Mari patted her shoulder. "Well, that's only natural. You'll be meeting his family and friends for the first time. You'll stun them all."

Delilah appreciated the small talk between her and her friend as she waited for Ash. It helped her feel grounded and reminded her that she still had her own world outside of the madness of his underworld. The doorbell chimed and they both scurried from her bedroom.

She opened the front door and there he stood, every inch of him devastating in his black tux. Her lips curved in a tiny smile as she grabbed his hand and pulled him inside. His gaze shifted to

Mari standing right behind her and he gave her a small smile, extending his hand.

"You must be Mari. I know how close you and Delilah are and I thank you for being here with her tonight."

"Oh, of course. I wouldn't have missed helping her dress tonight for anything."

Delilah noted in amusement the star struck look on her best friend's face and cleared her throat. She stepped forward, wrapped an arm around Ash's waist, and gave him an adoring look that wasn't all play acting. "I think you have Mari's approval."

"If she's partly responsible for how beautiful you look tonight, she has my approval, too." He kissed the top of her head.

"Oh, yes. I told her how stunning she looks," Mari responded with a big smile. She turned to Delilah. "Well, I've done my job here and it's time for me to take off. Have fun tonight, you two. Call me when you get a chance and we'll get together for lunch." She exchanged a meaningful look with her friend.

Delilah followed her to the door and Mari gave her an enthusiastic two thumbs up before heading down the concrete path. She turned to find Ash's heated gaze focused on her. He closed the distance between them and pulled her into the strong band of his embrace. His kiss was rough, and she submitted, parting her lips for him. After a moment, she pulled away, rubbing her lips gently. "There goes my perfect lipstick job."

Ash laughed softly. "That's going to happen a lot when we're together. Are you ready to go?"

Delilah nodded and grabbed up her wrap and small, silver bag. "Let's do this."

———

Delilah stood at the entrance of the lavishly decorated ballroom with a red and black theme. Long dining tables were covered in the colors, with decorative scented candles on each one. Sheer red and black drapes hung from the ceiling, creating a dramatic effect. She stood next to Ash as he shook hands with members of the underworld council. His elders didn't worry her, though she had expected to be more nervous about them. Her nerves were on edge because of a pair of eyes she felt on her.

During a break in the well wishes, she gritted her teeth and shot her husband a dark look. She kept her voice at a whisper, knowing full well he could hear every word and her heartbeat, if he tried. "Ash, I'm going to ask you this one time only. Why is your queen shooting daggers at me with her eyes?"

Ash smiled and shook another hand in the moving line. His expression never slipped. "Galina was my lover many decades ago when I was newly turned. She's still exceedingly jealous."

"Why does that not surprise me?" Delilah maintained her smile, nodding politely at another council member. She knew she did indeed looked stunning in a black, full length, strapless gown with black high heels but something about the way Galina carried herself in her crimson dress left her feeling second fiddle. "Is there a chance you'll find your way back to her bed?"

"No and we'll talk about this later." He settled a possessive arm around her shoulders as Galina approached and Delilah gladly leaned into him, uncomfortable under the queen's focused stare.

———

Ash kept his face carefully blank as the queen stood in front of him. "Queen Galina. Thank you for joining us this evening for this special celebration. I know how busy you are."

"Ah, Ash and the lovely new wife, Delilah." Galina unwound a crimson ribbon from her wrist, smiling. "Aren't you radiantly beautiful, my dear?" Her face was a serene mask, but her eyes burned with hatred. He instinctively moved closer to Delilah and focused his hearing on her thumping heartbeat. He knew this whole experience was a torment for her.

The queen summoned the council members to form a circle

around them. "It's time for the blessing of this union, under the protection of the Crown. Please, Ash, hold your wife's hand."

Ash took her hand in his. Galina wrapped the ribbon around their wrists and spoke a few words in their traditional language. The council members bowed their heads and repeated her. She made the sign of a crucifix over their joined hands. Delilah eyes widened, startled when the queen kissed her forehead.

Galina's grin was sly, and Ash's belly clenched in dread. He was confident that he was a few steps ahead of her but there was still a lingering fear. He knew exactly what the bitch was capable of.

"Welcome to our family, even as unexpectedly as it happened. A smart man knows to keep his treasure hidden." She turned to Ash. "I must return to the airport. I'm needed back in Denver immediately. I'll be in touch." She floated away.

William approached them and extended his hand to Ash. "I was more than surprised to hear that you had tied the knot, old friend." He smiled at Delilah and she flashed a smile of her own. "It warms my heart to know that you are now a part of our underworld and you'll be a good wife to Ash." He winked. "He's been alone in this life for far too long."

William clapped Ash on the back. "I understand how you couldn't be without her." His expression sobered. "Regarding that important matter we have to discuss, I'll just need to borrow you from your wife for a few minutes."

Ash nodded. "Most definitely." He kissed Delilah's cheek and left her with a parting smile.

William chose one of the back rooms in the banquet hall, all the way to the rear of the building. They stepped inside, and William closed the door firmly, looking directly at Ash. He shook his head slowly. "None of this is good news, my old friend," William said. "I know I asked you to play only a small part for the moment in this game with Galina. However, I have received some important intel regarding Romanov and we need your strength and your cunning."

Ash tensed up, every one of his senses sharp at the thought of taking down Romanov tonight. "Tell me everything. Where do you need me?"

"I've received information about two young women, barely out of their teens, being held in the back room of one of Galina's Los Angeles clubs. We need to organize an ambush to rescue them and I would like you to spearhead it. If we can successfully stop Romanov, this will simply be more evidence to take the queen down. We're equipping your whole crew with body cameras to document everything."

Ash stroked his bristled chin. "Excellent strategy. I'm ready. When do we make our move?"

William nodded. "I assume you'll be escorting Delilah home. Your crew will pick you up from there in one of the vans."

The two men left the room and headed back down the plush carpeted hallway. Ash spotted Delilah across the room, talking to the vamp Chyna. Both women stopped speaking and turned as Ash approached them. He tipped his head at the female vamp. "Chyna, good to see you. It's been a while."

She gave him a broad smile. "Ash, how lovely to see you again. I was just acquainting myself with your new wife. I'm sure Galina is pleased to have someone new become a part of our happy little vamp family in her kingdom."

Ash knew she was both fishing for information and mocking his affair with Galina. Conversation over. He grasped Delilah's hand. "I'm sure my wife will fit in just fine. We really have to go." He hastily guided her away.

Delilah turned to him, eyes narrowed. "I'm ready to call it a night. Before that, we need to have a talk."

He placed his hand in the small of her back and guided her back to their dining table to collect their things. "Not here. There are far too many listening ears." He guided her outside and to the car. "I want you to have your privacy, but I need to remain close to you every moment."

Heavily flanked by her security guards, Galina stood outside waiting for her car. The click of high heels signaled someone approaching and she spun around quickly. Her eyes narrowed, and she wasn't surprised to see Chyna. "What do you want?" she snapped, her patience with the vamp and her games worn thin.

Chyna inclined her head. "I'm here to talk business. I understand you're blocking my acquisition of the building to house my second boutique."

The queen nodded, wearing a smirk. "Indeed, I am. I have plans to utilize that prime piece of real estate for something more important than your silly clothing."

The other vamp's face twisted, and she clipped her words. "That 'silly clothing' is how I make my living. I've been working out the details for that building for months."

Galina shrugged. "And, now you're not. Find somewhere else to put your store." Her limousine pulled up and she waved Chyna away dismissively. One of the security guards quickly opened the back door for her and she settled in, leaving the other vamp standing outside and smiled.

When her cell phone chirped, she immediately recognized the voice on the other end of the call as her associate, Romanov. "This is only a slight wrinkle in our plans. You will have your human servant delivered to you, as promised in exchange for forgiving the debt. I'm the queen and ultimately, what I want is the law of the land. Don't concern yourself with Lockler. I'll take care of everything." She abruptly ended the call, leaning back against the plush seat with a satisfied sigh.

The last name McDade. Galina had been turning it over in her mind all evening after her first glimpse of the bride. She remembered Martin McDade well as the weak, desperate drunk who couldn't keep a dollar in his pocket for his gambling addiction. There was another younger McDade involved in the often seedy underworld who also was too eager to place bet after bet and throw away money on whores.

She smiled to herself, supremely satisfied now that she had

made the connection. She would wager her undead life that the bride Delilah, the younger man McDade, and Martin were all family, no doubt his children. The resemblance was striking. She also strongly suspected that Ash was aware of it. The queen had ground Martin's life into fine dust with a phone call and a bullet and now she was presented with his precious daughter to use as a pawn. Galina enjoyed the irony of the situation. Playing with human lives was entertainment to her and, after her next move, no one would be amused except her.

———

Dalilah nodded in understanding, knowing now how dangerous the underworld. She wasn't going to fight him on that issue anymore. "So, you'll be staying with me at night?"

"Yes, and during the day, I'll be resting in the home right across from you. I've leased it for the next six months. Your guards will be on watch twenty four/seven."

She wrung her hands in worry. "What about Declan?"

"He's under my protection just like I promised you and he's well-guarded in Seattle." He shrugged off his suit jacket

Delilah met his eyes squarely. "Am I in imminent danger from your queen?"

Ash shook his head. "I can handle Galina. She may be poisonous, but she wouldn't dare to make such a bold move with you now as my wife."

She arched an eyebrow. "You slept with her when you were newly turned. I assume it was a love affair that ended badly. Is that why she keeps trying to punish you?"

"Largely, yes." He sighed heavily. "You should also know that I'm in servitude to the Crown and the council. I-I killed my maker, Delilah. That's a serious crime among vampires. We deeply value life, including human."

"So, you're not an enforcer by choice? Galina is forcing you to risk your life while doing her dirty work because you ended a life?

That makes no sense to me." She shook her head slowly. "Why did you kill your maker?"

"Because he was a cruel, twisted bastard who liked to hurt women."

"Then, of course, you did the right thing." She crossed her arms and pinned him with her gaze. "Now, back to Galina. Do you still want her? Do you love her?"

Ash shrugged. "I thought I loved her a long time ago. She was a fantasy I endangered my life chasing after. The reality of her is stifling and oppressive. Her love is a trap and I didn't see that when I was younger. Come on, Delilah. Galina and I were over and done with decades ago. No more questions."

She looked down at the floor. "I sound like a jealous shrew."

He cupped her face in his hands. "While I'm sleeping with you, there won't be anyone else. I can promise you that. I don't know about this thing between us that has me twisted in knots, this need to possess you in every way and take care of you. Let's just see where it leads, all right?"

She covered his hand with hers. "I used to feel so alone in this world before I met you. You're like some fairytale guy who's too good to be true at the end of the story. Can we just hold each other tonight?"

Ash gave her a little smile, hugging her close to his chest. "I think it's been ages since some man held you close. Let me do that later on tonight, honey. I have some business to handle but I'll be back there with you in a few hours." He kissed the top of her head.

"Is this more of your enforcer work?"

"It is, but I promise you're safe and I'll be back soon."

She lowered his head and whispered into his ear. "Come back to me. Be safe, Ash."

———

Ash sat in the back of the van, a crossbow on his lap. He had a crew of eight, including the driver. All of them were dressed in black, heavy clothing and wore ski masks. His second in command on this ambush, Jason, tapped his shoulder. "Galina had the old back door at Club Dare replaced a few weeks ago. It's a lot heavier now with a bunch of reinforced heavy wood and steel."

"In that case, I imagine it will take our whole crew to bust it down, but we have to save those girls."

His second nodded. "I hear you on that. You've been away from this type of work with the rest of us for a long time. We missed you, bro." The two bumped fists.

Ash chuckled. "The only thing I want right now is to be finally free of Galina and I'm prepared to do whatever it takes."

The driver called out over his shoulder. "Five minutes away from Club Dare. Let's get ready, guys."

Ash carefully inspected his crossbow as they pulled into the large parking lot of the club. "Keep us a safe distance from the back exit. We're going to do this in waves. I'm heading wave one of the attack with four of us and Jason will lead the rest of you in blocking all access to escape vehicles in the parking lot. No vamp in that back room leaves here alive, understand?"

The crew in the back with him muttered in agreement. As the van came to a rolling stop, Ash and his small band jumped out and raced towards the back exit. They each took their positions as deftly and silent as ninjas. Ash approached the door, trying the handle first. Locked. He motioned for two of his small crew to help him and they flanked behind him. He gave another signal and they launched a full mode attack on the door's reinforcements.

Within moments, a barrage of bullets came from inside and pierced the door. Gunfire would never kill a vamp but they sure as hell left a nasty wound. Ash and his crew kept working on getting the door down. He admitted to himself that this new door was formidable, even to a vamp. After long strenuous minutes, they were able to crack the wood and bend the frame.

They entered the back room of the club and came face to face with two vamps wielding machine guns. The young women stood in a corner, holding on to each other, both sobbing. Ash could see the multiple bruises on their arms and his fangs shot out in a sudden burst of anger. He focused his gaze on the two vamps who were their captors. "They're not your property anymore. They're mine." He lifted his crossbow. "You fucks got a problem with that?"

One of them sneered. "Yeah, I got a big problem with that." He lifted his machine gun and before he could squeeze off a round, Ash sent an arrow whizzing through the air into his head dead center. The other captor made a dive towards the entrance that led into the club as the first vamp disintegrated into dust. One of Ash's crew moved with lightning speed and jumped on the back of the fleeing vamp. He gored him deeply in the back with a wooden stake and he also disintegrated.

Ash turned his attention to the visibly trembling, scantily dressed young women and dropped his crossbow. He noted with disgust that they appeared to be barely out of their teens. He approached them slowly, with raised hands. One of them whimpered loudly.

"I'm not here to hurt you or keep you captive like them. My crew and I are here to rescue you. We're going to put you in our van and transport you to a safe place."

The women gave each other a look. The one with the dark hair cleared her throat and spoke softly. "How do we know we can we trust you?"

"You don't," Ash said flatly. "Would you rather stay here and wait for more hired guns to rush this back room? Honestly, they'll be here in just a few minutes."

Both shook their heads and moved as one closer to Ash.

"Believe me, you're safe now."

They rushed him in an instant, clinging to him and sobbing. He held them tightly for a few moments and motioned for one of his crew members.

"This is my comrade and he's going to escort you to the van with our driver."

Ash's walkie-talkie squawked, and Jason spoke. "Hey, man. We need you all back outside. We ran into Galina's security team and we've got a fight going."

He grabbed up his crossbow and followed his comrade with the two women to the van. His crew exited the back room behind him and preparing their weapons. At Ash's hand gesture, they all shot out in a blur from behind the vehicle. In a flash, he surveyed the parking lot where five henchmen were ready to battle. Jason's crew of four moved into formation along with Ash and his crew to move as a unit, storming the parking lot.

Ash ignored the barrage of gunfire and slinging arrows, focused solely on the kill. One of the vamps rushed him in a tackle. He fought to stay on his feet and grabbed him around the neck, crushing bones. The vamp fell to his knees and Ash quickly leveled the crossbow, shooting an arrow into his chest. He exploded into dust that blew away in the night breeze.

The battle was fierce and short with the crew annihilating all the henchmen. The chilly wind picked up, dusting the whole parking lot with greasy ashes. Jason came to Ash and the two vamps shook hands. "Good fight, old man."

Ash chuckled. "Soon, I'll be eating off the senior menu in a roadside café, I reckon. I couldn't have done this without you and the rest of the crew. Come on, let's get the young ladies to safety and call it a night. I have a wife to go home to."

———

Later, Ash stood under the warming jets of water in Delilah's shower. His mind kept returning to the young women held captive by Romanov and Galina's team in the back of the vampire nightclub. He couldn't stop thinking about his wife in their place, bound and helpless at Romanov's mercy. Time to step up his own security team keeping watch over her. Their marriage may be just a business arrangement, but he had sworn to protect her and her brother. He smiled as her lilting voice sang along with the blaring music she had put on. Delilah was worth holding onto.

When she was soundly asleep in his embrace a few hours later, his thoughts turned again to Gentry, his maker. The older vamp had never been less than jovial and courteous to those who didn't know him well, but Ash remembered him better as the predator he was, sexual and otherwise.

Los Angeles, California, the past

The red-light district cathouse was humming with business of the dirtiest kind this evening. Ash heaved a sigh as he reclined in the plush easy chair, his eyes trained again on a particularly busy whore. For lack of anything better to do, with his sexual appetite satisfied earlier by a heated session in her bed, he watched her travel upstairs several times with the finely dressed dandies. What in the hell was keeping Gentry?

He had survived as a newly made vampire, against the odds, for nearly ten years. Ten years spent secretly loathing everything about Gentry. The older vampire was just as cruel as he was charming, especially with women, and Ash longed to take his head clean off, on most days. He also didn't care for most other vampires he knew, many of them being Gentry's associates.

As far as Ash's parents knew, he had died tragically in an automobile accident, traveling to another farm for work. That whole business weighed heavily on him whenever he imagined them grieving at the loss of their only child. He was broken inside from his own grief.

Gentry appeared at the top of the staircase, his big hands gripping a young girl's hips as he moved her down the steps. Ash narrowed his eyes, a white-hot rage filling him. He was up from the chair like a shot and moving swiftly. He glared at him from the foot of the stairs, his words clipped. "I see what kept you." He turned his gaze to the smiling girl. "Shouldn't you be in bed for the night? School tomorrow?"

She clucked playfully, flipping her long dark hair back. "Oh, I was just having a bit of fun talking with Gentry while mama's busy. He knows to keep his hands to himself since I'm still the baby. I promise you both a real good time when I'm of age." She laughed as the older vamp sent her on her way with a hair ruffle. His tone was cold.

"What if I was plowing her?" he asked, coming down the stairs. "What business is that of yours?"

"The girl's only fifteen fucking years old! They seem to get younger, year after year, you low life bastard."

Gentry's hand shot out, delivering a punishing blow to Ash's cheek, and nearly knocking him to the floor. He heard the conversations close to them abruptly cease and looked up to see all eyes on him. He struggled to his feet. Crimson was all he saw for long moments and it occurred to him that the vicious blow had broken a few blood vessels in his eyes.

Fury overtook him as the older vampire chuckled, but he didn't charge him. Within seconds, he calmly grabbed up an ax from the fireplace and stood in front of Gentry. The large crowd quickly moved back as the two vampires circled each other.

"I've given you the entire world to satisfy you, Asher. You're a poor return on my investment."

Ash chuffed without a trace of humor. "You have given me nothing but years of misery." He expertly swung the ax back and forth. "This will finally be the best night of my existence as a predator."

Gentry grabbed the ax handle, giving Ash the leverage he needed to shove him to the ground. The older vamp wasn't fast enough to avoid his foot placed squarely on his chest. His expression changed into fear and desperation. He flashed a nervous smile. "Search your memories, son. Our family…haven't we had some good times? Surely, it's not all bad?"

Ash lifted the ax. "You've left a blemish on every good day I've ever had since I met you. I've been thinking recently that the way to end all that is to end you." He brought the sharp blade down with force, severing Gentry's head from his body. Greasy dust exploded in every direction, amid the loud gasps from the crowd.

Ash heaved a deep breath and the ax fell at his feet. He undid his tie and wiped his gritty face with his shirt sleeve. He wore a crooked smile as he slowly walked to the open front door. He gave the crowd one last look. "Your little girls are a hell of a lot safer now." He was gone from the front porch before they could blink.

Ash smiled in the darkness, the memory no longer painful and bitter. "Best day ever," he murmured to himself. He stroked Delilah's hair, inhaling the fresh perfume. She would never know Gentry, and for that, he was grateful to whatever God was above for vampires.

SEVEN

Late the next afternoon, Delilah puttered around her home. Neither TV nor reading held her interest very long. The radio was on softly in the background. She wondered how Ash was faring in the home across from hers, knowing he would be awake when dusk came. She was all fluttery with excitement to spend time with him. Her curiosity soon got the better of her and she stepped outside, keys to his place in her hand, and closed her front door behind her.

She unlocked his door and crept in quietly so as not to disturb his rest. Every shade was drawn and in the near darkness, she could make out his sleeping form on the black leather sofa. One of his arms covered his face and he was perfectly still. She marveled that his chest didn't move with his breaths. He had several open duffel bags filled with his clothing in the corner and she bent down to inspect closer.

She stealthily pulled out a pair of his old faded jeans and rubbed the softened material against her cheek and caught a whiff of his expensive cologne. His simple jeans and T-shirt look, with the beat up leather jacket, was so masculine and so Ash. She folded his jeans over one arm and made her way out of the place.

Leaning back against the front door of her home, she cradled her find to her chest. She smiled to herself as she stripped off the lounging dress she wore and slipped into his jeans, which were far too big for her small frame. She went to her bedroom and pulled out an old grey T-shirt. She slipped it on and found a belt in her closet to cinch around her waist.

Inspired, she quickly set up her painting easel. She was far from a professional, but she loved to dabble with water color art in whatever spare time she had. She had requested a few weeks off from her job to get settled in her new life, so she now had nothing but time on her hands. She set up her subject, a colorful bowl of fruit on the table, and went to work.

————

Ash dressed himself comfortably, having just showered and prepared himself to feed for the evening. Even though willing human donors were very hard to come by, he saw no need to take blood from Delilah, though he very much wanted to. Animal blood would have to suffice. He recalled how he had marked her breast that first night and he went hard. Though she was her own woman and independent as hell, he still wanted to leave his mark of possession on her. He would happily take down any vamp that ever wanted to lay claim to his new wife in the future.

He closed the door to his place and rapped firmly on her door as he realized he had forgotten his set of keys to her place. She opened the door with a small smile, beckoning him to come in. He was intrigued when she sat down at an easel, picking up a small paint brush.

She looked up. "Hi. Did you rest well?"

Her jeans caught his attention and he realized, with the smell of his cologne filling his sensitive nose, they were his own. He gestured at them. "How did you get—"

She wrinkled her nose playfully. "I stole a pair of your jeans while you were sleeping. They just looked comfortable."

He laughed, shaking his head. "Fine with me. It could've been worse. You could've had your way with me while I was asleep."

She giggled as he came to stand behind her, looking at her water color art. "Hey, you're pretty good at that."

"I'm just a dabbler. I do it mainly to relax and keep myself occupied when I get bored."

He cleared his throat. "Um, I need to feed and handle some other business so please promise me you'll stay here behind locked doors while I'm gone. It'll be a few hours. One of my security guys will be keeping watch."

Delilah nodded. "I'll be fine. I know you prefer blood to actual food, but I'll make us some cupcakes while you're gone and have them waiting for you. Chocolate ok?"

"Hm. Chocolate is a weakness of mine." He tilted her chin up and kissed her soundly. "Be back soon. Make sure everything is locked after I leave."

Before he gave into his other weakness—her—he turned and headed out the front door. He strode down the path that curved around to the parking area where his bike waited. His coming meeting with William had him amped at the prospect of Galina's destruction and his part in it.

————

The sunset's last vibrant rays filtered in through Delilah's bedroom window as she grabbed up freshly laundered clothes from the basket and folded them neatly. She had abandoned her painting in favor of a late meal with contents from her refrigerator. The cupcake project was her next thing to tackle, all the ingredients waiting for her on the kitchen counter.

She heard her front door open and then loud, bumping. She dropped the towel she had been folding onto the bed and headed down the long hallway to the front living area, anticipating Ash's return. She rounded the corner. "Ash, I didn't expect—" She locked eyes with a stocky stranger wearing a black ski mask. Her heart beat double time as she raced back down the hallway to her bedroom and tried to slam the door shut.

The muscular assailant pushed at the door and knocked her to the floor. She screamed as he grabbed her by her arms and easily scooped her up on his shoulder as if she were a sack of feathers. She clawed at his back as he carried her down the hallway to a waiting, second figure in black. Even as she fought, the other one gagged her and wrapped rope tightly around her wrists. He slipped a tight blindfold over her eyes. She heard them exchange words in a strange language as they carried her out of her home. Her heart pounded in terror and her mouth went dry.

Her panic exploded as she was shoved in the back of a vehicle and the door slid shut. It roared to life and jumped into motion. She tried to rise and jerked at the rope binding her wrists. Her efforts were futile. She drew up in the fetal position and tried to stop the hitch in her shallow breaths. No vision, gagged, and bound made her the perfect victim for whatever was coming.

Ash knew trouble had found them as he came around the corner to see a big pile of dust where his two posted guards had been standing a few hours before. His mind instantly switched gears from relaxed and happy to something far more predatory. His fangs sprang out prepared for a fight, his mind filled with images of a dead or hurt Delilah.

He found her front door open as his sensitive nose picked up the foreign scent of at least two vamps. Her scent lingered as he checked every room for any trace of her. The folded clothing on her bed told him she'd been doing the laundry when they had taken her. His heart hurt to imagine her terrified confusion.

His gut reaction was to track her right away on his own. He reigned in his impulse, instead coolly calculating his next move. This was Galina's work. His queen was paying him back by defiantly snatching his wife. He remembered William's words to him earlier about Galina being under constant surveillance until they had enough information and proof to end her corrupt empire. He knew instantly who his first call should be. He grabbed his cell phone from the pocket and tapped the screen.

"William, we've got big trouble. Delilah's been taken."

———

Delilah stayed perfectly still in her seated position on the carpeted floor in a corner. She was still bound, gagged, and blindfolded and she dared not attract attention to herself. Vamps moved quietly so she couldn't be sure she was alone in whatever room she was in. She wasn't the hysterical type in the face of danger, but her fear was overwhelming, and she shivered. She knew if Ash didn't find her, she would be forced to save herself if that was even possible.

The door's lock scraped, and her heart thudded. Next came the sound of footsteps that stopped right in front of her. She remained frozen in position, afraid to move. She heard a feminine voice.

"Please...please, let me go home. I have a family probably already looking for me since I haven't called them to check in."

Delilah felt the woman roughly shoved down beside her. Her blindfold and gag were removed, and she blinked a few times under the harsh fluorescent lighting. She looked beside her as the guard also removed the other woman's blindfold. The other captive was dark haired with the face of very young woman, no doubt just out of her teens. Their eyes met.

The guard leaned down into their faces. "I'll be back to bring you some things. You two are going to stay bound up." He left, slamming the heavy door.

Tears streaming down the young woman's face and Delilah instinctively took her hand tightly. "I know you're scared. I am, too. My name is Delilah. What's yours?"

She held on. "I'm Bindi and I'm an idiot for thinking that clubbing alone was a good idea."

Delilah smiled gently. "They snatched you at a vamp club, I assume?"

Bindi nodded. "I didn't know what it was at the time. I just followed a hot guy-vampire inside when he gave me a free pass. My friends claimed they had met some real-life vampires and I could meet some cute ones visiting Club Dare." She smiled shyly. "Is that where they got you, too?"

She shook her head slowly, her heart hurting for innocent Bindi. "No. My story is more complicated than that. I'm married to a vamp, but he's a good man. I was snatched by the vampire queen to punish him."

Bindi's eyes went wide. "You married one? Wow. Does he know where you are?"

She nodded. "I'd stake my life on it." Her lips curved upwards. "Sorry. Poor choice of words. My husband, Ash, is probably looking for me right now. Speaking of stakes, I see nothing in this room that would make do as one." She sighed. "And, we're heavily guarded."

Bindi shook her head. "My parents are going to freak out when I'm not back home in the morning." She looked up at Delilah. "Is there any chance that your vampire husband will fight to get you back and save me, too?"

She patted the younger woman's hands in comfort. "Bindi, there's a hundred percent chance of that."

The door's lock scraped again, and the same guard entered the room, carrying two sets of blue scrubs and white flip flops. He tossed them at their feet and motioned for them to stand up. Delilah's knees cramped from sitting for so long and she swore under her breath.

"I'm undoing your restraints so that you both can change your clothes. There's another guard right outside so I wouldn't try to escape, if I were you." He pointed at Delilah. "I'm escorting you somewhere else, so hurry up."

She exchanged a worried look with Bindi as her heart dropped in dread. After the guard left the room, both women hastily undressed and changed into the scrubs and flip flops. He returned a few minutes later and roughly grabbed Delilah's arm, swinging her around. He blindfolded her again and secured her restraints, before leading her from the room.

Delilah whispered a little prayer for her and Bindi as the guard escorted her down a hallway and into another room. The silence was deafening, and her nerves were wrecked as she waited to see what new horror was ahead. It could've been ten minutes, or it could've been an hour.

A door opened, and she remained still. She gave no indication she knew someone else was in the room, until the restraints were removed. Next, came the blindfold and she was looking at a face she didn't know. He was tall, thin, with a hook nose and had a head of grey hair pulled back into a long ponytail. His fangs were out, and he smiled wolfishly.

"Welcome, servant. I am Romanov and I own you now. I expect obedience from you. You are to do nothing without my permission, understood?"

Delilah said nothing, keeping her eyes downcast. He grabbed her chin roughly. "Stubborn, I see. Good. I expect you'll be as spirited and defiant in my bed, which is good as you'll be spending a lot of time there. Until, of course, I grow bored with you." He grabbed a handful of her hair. "We won't be staying here for too much longer. Soon, you'll be prepared for transport to my home in Alaska, where you will live out your short, pathetic human life serving me in many ways."

In a flash of memory, she recalled Ash telling her what Galina had planned for her. Her temper got the better of her at the idea that she would be anyone's servant. "Don't touch me!" she hissed. "I'm Ash Lockler's wife and you won't get away with treating me like this. He'll hunt you down and stake you for even touching me. Before he takes you out, he'll make you hurt."

Romanov barked out a laugh. "By the time Lockler tracks you down, it'll be far too late to save you. You'll be beaten down and broken until you live to serve and pleasure only me."

She shook her head, her expression fierce. "That will never happen. I will never want you."

He slapped her hard across the face and she tasted blood. His next words chilled her.

"There will be many more lessons like that until I've broken you completely. He won't even want you anymore. You'll be of no use to him."

Left alone, with her eyes tearing up, she whispered, "Please hurry up and find me, Ash."

A moment later, the same guard ushered her back to the first room. When he removed the blindfold, disappointment filled her. Bindi was gone.

————

Ash replayed the day of Delilah's disappearance over and over in his mind as he stretched out on her sofa in the dark. He had failed her as a protector. Everything he'd promised wouldn't happen to her had, in the worst way. She had been missing for two days and he was now forced to seriously reflect on exactly what she meant to him. His only experience with love had been the disastrous affair with Galina when he was young and thought he knew what love was. He had come to realize, after genuinely caring for Delilah over the past few months, that what he felt for Galina was nowhere even close to the target. Where Galina was selfish and needy, Delilah was warm, generous, and affectionate. *I love her, but I let her down.*

His cell phone rang, and he immediately tapped the screen to answer, praying for mercy from God and news about her. "William. Any updates?"

The elder's voice was laced with concern. "I know you and your own men have been out there searching for her, but now is the time to call it off. The few council members who are on our side have rallied with me and we have found your wife."

Ash heaved relieved sigh before cursing loudly. "Romanov is

twisted and loves to abuse women. Where are they? I'm going to make sure he suffers the final death and bring her home."

"This is all Galina's doing, of course. Delilah was sold to settle one of her debts to the bastard. Before you head out to get her, you should know that we have one of his security guards willing to sell Galina out in exchange for leniency from the council."

"Give me all the details so I can make a game plan for her rescue."

"Yes, Ash, let's pull this plan together. We don't have much of a window to get her back before Romanov disappears with her."

———

Delilah was finally free of her restraints and waited nervously on a sofa in the bare white room. By her calculations this must be the evening of day three of her captivity. She desperately wanted to do more than quickly brush her teeth and shower for longer than three minutes at a time. Her captors had separated her from Bindi and she prayed she would survive this. There was no way in hell she would leave the place without the younger woman.

Two armed guards, both vamps, stood by the door, dashing her hopes of simply making a run for it. She had kept herself calm, coolly assessing her chances of making a quiet escape during the change of guards but, so far, there had been zero opportunity. One of the guards approached her, smirking. He fondled her breasts and she pushed at his hands, cringing in disgust. Her slap ripped across his face and he swore loudly, swinging his arm to backhand her.

The other guard clasped his shoulder, pulling him back. "Hey, no touching the merchandise. She belongs to Romanov. Respect that or face the consequences of his anger."

The first guard narrowed his eyes. "I just wanted a quick sample. I guess, like with all the others, he'll get tired of her and pass her on to us."

"Go check on the details for her transport tonight. I want a full update on the progress."

The grabby handed guard gave her one last leering look before following orders and leaving the room. She turned to the remaining guard. "Thank you for that. It's bad enough being a captive, stuck in this hell, but him touching me…"

His voice dropped lower as he met her gaze. "Help often comes when you least expect it." Unexpectedly, he winked. He moved to speak right in her ear. "Don't drink whatever they give you in those water bottles later."

Delilah's heart lifted with joy. Somehow, she had managed to find an ally and her gut told her Ash was behind it. Her smile was tremulous as the guard left the room.

———

Ash pulled the ski mask on. He was seated in a surveillance van with a small crew of four vamps. Jason, his comrade, was the driver. He checked his crossbow. It was ready for action. He had another weapon, a sharp stake, in the waistband of his pants. "Jason, what do you have from your viewpoint up there?"

"Still a lot of activity in and out of the compound. I'll bet tonight's the night for transporting all the women, including your wife. Check your mike, man. Can you hear me?"

Ash checked his equipment, including the body armor camera that would, hopefully, record the rescue mission. "I'm solid, man. I need you to be my eyes and ears here outside, instead of in the fight."

He slid the van's door open and stepped out, gesturing his crew into position.

Ash stealthily approached the old building that served as Romanov's compound on the outskirts of Hollywood. Dressed in black, including the ski mask, he hoped to blend in with the security detail inside. He gripped the handle on one of the back doors, breaking it with considerable effort. Once inside, he looked down one of the two long hallways, remembering the building layout from the blueprint William had given him. They had probably moved her, but he crept down the left hallway in hopes he wasn't too late.

He checked all the rooms in the left hallway, coming up empty. Damn, they had moved her. He made his way back down to the fork at the front and continued down the right hallway.

Just as he reached the door to the first room, an armed vamp guard came around the corner. Ash gave him a nod. "Just checking on the prisoners."

The guard returned the nod. "They're about an hour away from transport. Romanov will be down soon." He walked down the hallway and disappeared around the corner. Ash broke the lock on the door and cracked it open an inch, coolly surveying. He pushed it open further, a wave of relief washing over him to see Delilah looking at him apprehensively from her place on a sofa. He stepped inside and closed the door behind him. Before she could speak, he pulled the ski mask off and shushed her with a finger to his lips.

Her face lit up with joy and she raced to him. She wrapped her arms tight around his waist and he dropped the crossbow to hold her to him, kissing the top of her head. He buried his nose in her hair, remembering her unique sweet scent. He smelled something else, just below her scent but couldn't place it. He whispered in her ear. "I'm as good as my word, honey. I meant what I said about keeping you safe, and don't worry, your brother is fine."

She nodded, tears filling her eyes. She stroked his face with her fingertips. He touched the faint bruise on her jawline gently and swore under his breath. "He put his hands on you? Did he hurt you…in any other way?"

She shook her head. "He slapped me but nothing else." She grabbed his arm. "Don't leave without Bindi. She's just an innocent girl. This place is a living hell and I'm sure Alaska with Romanov is ten times that."

"We won't leave without her, honey. I promise."

He bent to kiss her just as the door exploded inward. Romanov stalked in, his expression feral.

"It's very unfortunate that you're here to reclaim your human. That move will cost you your life tonight, Lockler."

Ash was overwhelmed with a surge of anger and adrenaline, his fangs out. He would show the older vampire no mercy for even thinking about Delilah. "She's my wife and that still means a hell of a lot in our world, Romanov. I could reveal your crimes to the council and let them handle you, but I think I'm just going to kill you."

He lifted an eyebrow. "And risk another one hundred years of servitude or, perhaps, even your own life? Your word against mine."

Ash took a protective stance in front of Delilah. "It'll be well worth it."

Romanov moved in, his fangs exposed. Ash was on him before he could get closer. He knocked the older vamp to the floor and stepped on his throat. Romanov caught Ash's ankle and twisted, causing Ash to stumble backward. Lunging up, Romanov used his advantage, punching Ash repeatedly in the gut. Caught off guard by the blows, Ash went to his knees, taking a vicious kick to the face but pushed up to his feet. He rushed the older vamp and tackled him to the floor. He quickly straddled him, reaching in his waistband for his stake.

Romanov's smile was evil. "Do it and you'll be damned for your living eternity. No woman, human or otherwise, is worth that."

Ash focused on Delilah and the split-second cost him his leverage. The older vampire head butted him. He fell back, clutching his forehead, the stake falling from his hand. Romanov sprang up, planting his foot firmly on Ash's throat with a lopsided grin.

"This is the sad end to Galina's enforcer." Romanov snatched up the stake and lowered himself to right above Ash's chest. "I'll be fucking your wife over and over as your ashes blow in the wind outside, Lockler."

"Hey," Delilah called out. "I don't see that happening, you scum bastard."

Ignoring her, he sneered and raised the stake above Ash's chest. In the next second, an arrow shot from the crossbow and landed dead center in the older vamp's head. His expression was comically frozen disbelief before he disintegrated into large plumes of dust.

Ash wiped the mess from his face. Stumbling to his feet, he grabbed a trembling Delilah around her waist as his crossbow slipped from her hands. "Don't be scared. I have you, now. You're safe, honey." She clung to him and he felt like a hero for once in his long life. He murmured in her ear, "You're an excellent shot with that bow for a first timer. Come on, we need to get moving to find the other captives, including your Bindi."

He grabbed her hand and led her out of the room and down the hallway towards the back door. When they reached the fork, an explosion ripped through the other hallway. Ash instinctively put Delilah behind him to shield her from the surging heatwave and flying debris. He used his mic to call Jason. "What's happening?"

It squawked in his ear as his comrade spoke. "I'm still running surveillance outside but your team of four is already in the building looking for the captives. With that explosion, I'd guess things are heating up." He chuckled as Ash snorted.

"Sorry. Bad pun. Is Romanov burning in Hell yet?"

Ash barked a laugh. "He won't ever put his hands on another woman. Hey, man, I'm handing my wife off to you. Come to the back door on the east side."

Delilah clung to him, shaking her head. 'No! I don't want to leave you in here."

He wrapped his arm around her. "You're a tough shot with a crossbow and you did kill Romanov, but this mission is my responsibility. I can't fully focus with you here." He kicked open the bent back door and Jason stood outside. He pushed her into his comrade's waiting arms just as another explosion shook the building. "Go on, honey. You're safe."

He swiftly headed down a hallway and almost crashed into one of his team members rounding the corner, escorting a band of sobbing female captives. "Is this all of them?"

"There are a few more women located in the back rooms of this place. Two of our teams are handling that."

Ash looked into the eyes of each captive. "Are any of you named Bindi?" When they all shook their heads, he clapped his hand on his comrade's back. "Nice job. Get these women outside and loaded onto the other van."

Moving down the hallway, his mind focused on the image of the blueprint to this place. He knew there were two additional rooms at the back and headed for the first one. "Bindi! Bindi, can you hear me? I need to get you out of here. Don't be afraid."

His sharp hearing detected small grunts coming from behind the locked door of the second room. He wasted no time bashing the hell out of the door until it fell inward. A young woman with dark hair, bound and gagged in the far corner of the room, struggled against her restraints and he moved to help her.

He removed the gag, asking, "Are you Bindi?"

She sucked in a deep breath, nodding. He raised her up with a firm grip and worked on loosening her ties. "Who are you?"

"I'm Delilah's husband, Ash." The bindings slipped to the floor and she took an unsteady step. He held her upright until she could get her bearings. "Let's get moving. The place is burning."

Bindi's eyes were wet with tears and she looked awestruck. "Delilah said you would come for us, but I thought she may be wrong," she murmured.

Ash smiled and wrapped his arm around her. She limped as he helped her down the long corridor, now filled with thick, deadly smoke. They slipped outside into the brisk night air, making their way across the compound to where the two vans were parked. Jason emerged from the surveillance vehicle, his dark hair blowing in the breeze, and Ash moved Bindi towards him.

Jason's voice was gruff. "You're safe with us. We're—"

Bindi launched herself into his arms, kissing his cheek. "You're the good vamps." She turned her gaze on Ash. "Thank you for saving me. I promise I'll never go to another vampire club as long as I live." She smiled. "I assume that Delilah is already safe?"

Ash nodded. "She's fine. Let's get you someplace safe to recuperate before we take you home."

Jason looped an arm around Bindi and led her to the waiting van as Ash headed towards the other one where Delilah waited for him. He couldn't stop the satisfied grin he wore. Romanov was dead under the best set of circumstances. His team all wore the body armor with the cameras on, including himself. Galina had finally hung herself and he felt damn great about it.

Ash ended his phone call with William, deeply satisfied that this finally meant the end of Galina's rotten empire. The elder ordered him to let the council members handle every detail of the queen's takedown. With news of Romanov's death was making the rounds, the corrupt queen quickly announced that Ash was to be charged. At the hearing held for Ash's new crimes against the Crown, her rule would come to an end.

Having Delilah back safely home with him was more than good. The thought of how close he'd come to losing her disturbed him. He had found love with her in his arms and he knew he'd gladly kill a hundred vamps to keep her safe. Her home was now surrounded by a mass of hidden vampire security provided by the council. Light footsteps came down the hallway and she appeared around the corner. She wore a big, white, fluffy bath towel and a smile.

"It feels wonderful to be totally clean again. Just give me a few minutes to get dressed."

He caught a whiff of the strange scent again. "You smell different."

"I used a new body wash tonight."

Ash shook his slowly and moved closer to her. "No, it's something else that I noticed before." He sniffed her, stopping suddenly at her midriff. He parted the towel and placed his ear to her belly. He could make a faint whoosh of what sounded like a tiny heart beat inside of her. He blinked in confusion for long moments before looking up at her with a small smile playing on his lips.

Delilah's brow was furrowed. "What's wrong?"

His voice was rough with emotion. "Did you recently sleep with someone else before our first night together?"

She shook her head. "No, there's only been you."

He cradled her face in his hands. "I'm almost sure there's a baby in there."

Delilah's mouth dropped open and her hand went immediately to her belly. "Good Lord. How sure is almost?"

"I've never impregnated anyone, so I only know a little about how this works. There are precious few children born from a human and vampire union but I'm pretty confident I'm right. I think you're carrying my dhampir. With them, you can normally detect a heartbeat weeks before you could with a human child."

Delilah went back down the hallway quickly, speaking over her shoulder. "I'll get dressed and we can make a quick trip to the drugstore for a pregnancy test."

He heard the door close, lost in his joyful thoughts as he stood there. A baby meant that everything had changed. There was no way she was going through her pregnancy and child rearing alone. He knew she cared for him but that wasn't exactly love. He was now determined to make her see that she needed him in her life permanently, as his wife for good. If she didn't already, he would make her love him.

———

Delilah and Ash sat on her bed, clasping each other's hands. He had barely said two words while they'd picked a couple of pregnancy tests from the multitude of choices in the drugstore aisle. She didn't sense anger from him but was confused by his silence. Her heart thumped, and butterflies circled in her belly as he looked at the clock on her nightstand.

"It's been ten minutes for both tests. You ready to check?"

Delilah's voice was husky and low. "Yes. Let's check the sticks."

They went into the bathroom together, with Ash keeping his hands on her hips from behind. Her hands trembled as she lifted the first indicator stick. She lifted the box with her other hand, carefully re-reading the directions before putting it down. They looked at the stick together. It was bright pink.

"Positive." Delilah leaned her head back against his shoulder, letting out a huge sigh. She reached for the other stick, again checking the directions on the back of the box. She knew exactly what the double line meant. "Positive again." She turned in Ash's embrace, holding him tightly around the neck as happy tears filled her eyes.

He spoke with his face buried against her neck. "I'm so happy it hurts right now. I know it sounds selfish, when I'm not even sure you want your life to change so drastically. A baby with me was not what you expected."

"Not expected but definitely wanted." She kissed him soundly before leading him back into the bedroom. "I've always wanted children." She dropped on the bed and he knelt at her feet, smiling faintly.

"I'm crazy in love with you, honey. It took almost losing you for good to make me think about it and come to the uncomfortable realization that it's always been you I was meant to love in this never-ending life."

Delilah stroked his cheek with her fingertips. "Good, because I'm just as crazy in love with you. I thought we would end up having long months of good sex and then part ways. It's been hard for me to not have complete control over our situation. I'm used to making all the decisions in my life and trying to do the same in my brother's. You swept in and took my life into your hands. I need to know is this just about you taking responsibility because I'm pregnant? You don't have to say what you don't mean to cushion the blow of you eventually walking out of my life."

He laced his hand with hers. "I don't sugarcoat shit—ever. I say exactly what I mean. There's an old Chinese myth that says everyone is born with a red string tied around their ankle, just as their fated mate has one tied around theirs. We vampires adopted this myth as traditional truth, which is why the blessing ceremony of marriage involves a crimson ribbon."

Delilah wiped a falling tear from her face. "That's beautiful, but do you believe in all that? I do. I believe that my ankle has always been tied to yours."

He nodded and met her gaze. "I've waited for it to be true for a hundred years. I want that crimson ribbon Galina wrapped around our wrists to mean more than I intended because everything has changed. I will love you until I leave this life forever, onto whatever heaven awaits wicked vamps. I want to birth and raise our little baby together, loving each other passionately. I need to know are we on the same page? Do you want the life I've imagined for us?"

She wrapped her arms around his neck. "You're the only one I've ever wanted since you marked me that first night. You're right. The glamouring didn't make me do things I didn't want to do. It only lowered my inhibitions, making it easier for me to figure out my true feelings and act on them."

"I'm sorry I knocked you up. I didn't even think to use a condom, in case what I thought was impossible, actually happened."

She gave him a throaty laugh. "No, you're not. I think you're smiling in satisfaction over my shoulder because this miracle happened." She took his face in her hands. "I can't promise you an easy life with me deferring to your every request. I don't take demands well. We're bound to clash sometimes because we're remarkably alike in many important ways. You're as emotionally controlled as I am but I'm coming to understand that I can't live my life repressing what I feel."

He looked in her eyes and clasped her hand tightly. "I know it's terrifying to feel out of control but I'm happy you see it's ok to show me what's underneath. Later this week, you and I will face the council and Galina as husband and wife, to answer for my new crimes. Are you ready for that?"

She bowed her head. "Ash, I'm terrified for you."

His smile was enigmatic. "You'd be amazed if you only knew what's coming."

Later that night, they laid in each other's arms on the sofa in the dark, listening to music, with Ash's head resting on her belly. She was more than apprehensive but steadfastly clung to her faith that everything would work out.

———

"How can you be so calm about your trial? They won't execute you but what if Galina locks you away for the next hundred years and we never see each other again?"

"I'm fairly certain that won't happen, but if it did, I would always find my way back to you."

An hour later, Ash stood next to Delilah in the huge, dark room with only two lights in the ceiling, illuminating the dour faces of the Vampire Council and Queen Galina. The meeting room routinely served as a courtroom in one of the upscale hotels owned by vampires in Downtown Los Angeles. The seven council members, including William, sat at the large table and the queen stood at her podium. Another podium housed the electronic equipment, with a guard standing behind it, at the ready.

Ash clutched Delilah's hand for comfort. His gaze traveled to Galina across the room and she raised her eyes. Her lip curled slightly, her expression carefully blank. He knew her well, though, knew she was feeling triumphant at his situation. Another hundred years of servitude would ensure he would be firmly under her control. He looked away pointedly.

The queen's voice was clear and piercing. "Ash Lockler, even one hundred years of servitude sentence didn't deter you from killing another vampire. Romanov, who had a long life to look forward to, was savagely slaughtered by you." She pointed at the guard and he touched a few buttons on the projector. Suddenly, a huge image of Ash stealthily moving down the hallway of Romanov's compound filled the screen. "As you can all see, Lockler went on a mission of his choosing, without the Crown's permission, which resulted in Romanov's death at the hands of his human wife who, clearly, is not fit to be a part of the vampire kingdom. We vampires honor life, both ours and humans. Ash Lockler and his wife, Delilah, have no honor."

Ash let the video play without interruption, his jaw tensed in rage at how good Galina was at painting her own distorted interpretation of the facts. He calmed himself down. It would be no good to lose focus and give the game up in a fit of anger before the right moment came. The video ended, and the screen went dark.

"I was rescuing my wife from a sadistic vampire who had no regard for human or vampire life, one who got off on preying on women in the worst way. My wife stepped in to save me. His death was justified."

As Ash went silent, Galina's smile was pure evil. "The details on the supposed kidnapping are still murky so they will not be considered at this hearing." She turned to the council members. "After a careful review of all the evidence of Lockler's crimes that I have compiled and placed in the folders before you and the compelling video evidence, how do you each find the defendant?"

Ash squeezed Delilah's hand tightly and looked over at the guard at the podium. He nodded for the man to press a few buttons and the screen lit again. Galina froze when she recognized her own face and voice. The footage played on for long minutes, displaying different video clips from the body armor cameras. Each video clip of private business conversations was more incriminating than the last. The last clip captured Galina viciously staking another corrupt underworld business associate. The screen went dark and the silence was deafening.

William spoke first, his expression as stony and sober as the other elders. "What's more important here, Galina, is how we find you." He slammed his gavel down. "The queen is guilty." One by one, each elder condemned Galina as the security guards moved in quickly to grab her arms.

She shouted, her face contorted with rage. "You don't have any rights to condemn me. I am queen! I have the final word on all matters. Everything I've done has been to benefit the Crown and all vampires. What have you elders done except live in some dream utopia where you never have to get your hands dirty to protect and prosper? I'm untouchable!"

William's expression remained serene and unruffled. "Galina Saburova, we sentence you to blood draining until you are near the final death and burial for one hundred years. Whether you survive the punishment is of no concern to us. You have been stripped of your crown and we are in the process of dismantling your empire. You are exiled for the length of your eternity."

Galina's angry screams filled the room as she fought against the guards and Ash's lips curved in satisfaction. This was even better than he had imagined. More guards rushed the disgraced queen, restraining her as she hurled curse words at Ash and the council members.

"I won't forget who betrayed me here tonight! I will survive, and I promise you I will be back to destroy everyone in this room."

Chyna rose from her seat in the back of the room and strode towards Galina purposefully. As the guards restrained the queen, Chyna scratched her sharp nails across Galina's face, her own twisted in fury. She smiled darkly. "You underestimated me. I have eyes and ears everywhere which served me well to help take you down. My Dmitri's death has not gone unpunished, as well as the sins you committed against all those human girls. Enjoy your own private hell, bitch." She returned to the shadows of the room.

Delilah turned her gaze to meet Galina's. "You may survive your sentence, but my father never had a chance to live after you ordered his death. You have a hundred years of solitude to remember Martin McDade and his family, while we won't think of you at all."

Her smile bright and her eyes teary, Delilah looked at Ash. His own smile was small and tender.

"You were right. I am amazed. You got justice for my dad, Ash. Now he can finally rest. Thank you." She kissed his cheek.

They both watched as Galina was roughly escorted from the courtroom in shackles. The guards shoved her down the hallway as the door closed firmly behind them.

Each elder rose to shake Ash and Delilah's hands before leaving quietly through a side door. Only William was left and he heartily clapped Ash on the back, smiling. He lightly kissed Delilah on her cheek. "Mission extremely well accomplished."

Ash shook his hand. "Couldn't have accomplished much without you rallying the other council members to our cause. Thank you, for helping me save my wife."

Delilah nodded. "Yes, a deeply appreciative thank you. I was terrified out of my mind."

After a few moments of conversation, William bid them goodbye until the next council meeting and left the courtroom. Ash nodded at the lone guard at the podium. The guard smiled and gave him thumbs up before disappearing into the shadows.

Wrapping an arm around her shoulders, Ash led her out of the courtroom. "Ready to go home?"

"Yes, I need to chill out. My heart is still racing."

EPILOGUE

Delilah cradled her infant son with a loving smile as he gurgled. Christian was born after a long, excruciating labor, with Ash clutching her hand the whole ride. Because the baby was a dhampir, she'd birthed him in a vampire community hospital that could properly assist with the special needs of mother and son. He had snatched the hearts of both of his parents from the moment he made his arrival.

Christian grasped a lock of her long hair and she stroked his soft cheek. There was no doubt who his father was. Their baby strongly resembled Ash, right down to the vibrant green eyes. As a hybrid, time would eventually tell which vampire gifts he had inherited from his father. She looked up to meet Ash's gaze.

He took the baby from her and placed him in the carrier, with a kiss on his forehead. "Are you sure you want to do this? You don't have to change to make me happy, honey."

She waved her hand. "Of course I do. We're mated for life and I don't want to be an old lady on my deathbed in a few decades, leaving you and our child behind."

Delilah wore her favorite, black plush robe. She wanted to experience her changeover from human to vamp in something comfortable. Ash tugged her sleeve and she followed him out on the balcony of their lavish townhouse in Pasadena. She studied his face in the moonlight and rubbed his shoulder. "You have more doubts about this than I do. Even Declan has accepted my decision. I want to do it, so let's get started." She sat down on one of the recliners.

He searched her face for long moments before biting into his wrist. Crimson blood dripped, and he raised it to her lips. "This is your last moment before you become a part of forever, too." His voice was rough. "The change is going to hurt like hell, baby, but I'll be with you every minute."

She smiled gently and whispered, "Here goes." Without hesitation, she delicately licked his wound before sucking down his blood. Seconds ticked by with his gaze focused on her. An intense rushing of her own blood filled her ears, blotting out all other sounds. Her temples throbbed, and her vision narrowed to slivers. He caught her and carried her back inside to their bed. Every part of her body was heavy, and her eyes drooped. Severe cramps overtook her, from her feet to her head, and she screamed.

Ash embraced her as she thrashed, his whispers of concern in her ear. She lost track of time, slipping in and out of awareness. The burning all over her body was unbearable and, for a moment, she wished for death. She finally let it all go and gave in to the darkness.

———

His touch on her hypersensitive skin jerked her back awake. Soft fingers trailing across her cheek was a sensual delight and she opened her eyes. She was splayed out on their bed and Ash knelt beside her, smiling slightly. Her lips curved, and she grasped his hand. "Am I...done?"

He nodded. "You made it. I was worried you wouldn't survive the pain. Focus your hearing for a moment. Tell me what you hear."

Delilah could hear night time traffic, though it was miles away from their home in the hills. The rustling of leaves in the breeze, the whine of insects all sounded as clear as if she was standing outside. "I can hear everything," she gushed in excitement.

Ash pulled her into his arms. He lifted her lips and massaged her sore gums. Her eyes widened in surprise when her new fangs popped out. "How do I control them?"

He showed her for several moments how to extend and retract them until she was able to do it on her own. "Come on, let's go. There's an experience I don't want you to miss."

She frowned. "Where are we headed? And, what about the baby?"

"I called a sitter for an hour or two. She's already here. Get dressed and I'll meet you downstairs by my motorcycle."

She took her time dressing, marveling at her luminous skin and glowing eyes the changeover had brought. She zipped up her jeans and laced up her lug boots. The feel of her leather jacket against her skin had her shivering.

Delilah left instructions for the sitter and headed down the steps to where Ash stood next to his bike. He pulled her into his arms and planted a kiss on her lips before handing her the passenger helmet. She nimbly hopped on behind him and they took off into the night. Though the wind rushed loudly as they roared down the street, she could hear his every word.

"All of your senses are heightened. Take in every sensation as we ride. It's an unforgettable experience, baby."

She wrapped her arms around his waist and lost herself in the nocturnal beauty. The wind caressed her skin, a comfortable warmth despite the winter chill. The crystal clear bird songs in the trees seemed to be right in her ear. She looked up at the sky and realized she could see thousands more bright stars and a clearer, vibrant moon with her new vision.

As they rolled on, she marveled at the beauty of their life together. The council had given him a full pardon for his crime in killing his maker and relieved him of his role as the Crown's enforcer, welcoming him back into the legitimate fold. He now handled his various businesses exclusively. Delilah had left her position at KinderFun and headed her own child development consultant firm. They both set their own work schedules, which was the only way to deal with sleeping in the daylight hours.

Ash was every bit the vamp she had come to know well but there was always another layer of gentleness and humor to discover. She also adored the transition she'd made from human to vamp, reveling in her newfound abilities.

Ash brought them to a stop in the hills above their home. He killed the engine, propping the bike's kickstand before getting off. She got off and stood next to him, soaking in the beauty of the twinkling city lights spread out below them. She rested her head on his chest as he held her. "Thank you for my first ride as a vamp. It was amazing."

"I knew you would love it."

"You've gone from reckless player to a domesticated hubby, and papa in a relatively short time. I wonder if you have any regrets."

"Not a damn single one." He looked into her eyes. "I made you a kick ass vamp. Do you have any regrets?"

"Not when that means we have an eternity to love each other and parent our little guy. I love you with all of me, Ash." Her neat little fangs slid out. "Later, baby permitting, I'll show you just what I mean."

His grin was breathtaking as his eyes lit from an inner glow. "Ms. Prim is not so prim, as it turns out. Lucky me."

THE END

———

Don't miss out on your next favorite book!

Join the Satin Romance mailing list
www.satinromance.com/mail.html

THANK YOU FOR READING

———

Did you enjoy this book?

We invite you to leave a review at your favorite book site, such as Goodreads, Amazon, Barnes & Noble, etc.

DID YOU KNOW THAT LEAVING A REVIEW...

- Helps other readers find books they may enjoy.
- Gives you a chance to let your voice be heard.
- Gives authors recognition for their hard work.
- Doesn't have to be long. A sentence or two about why you liked the book will do.

ABOUT THE AUTHOR

Tamela Miles is a California State University San Bernardino graduate student with a Bachelor of Science degree in Child Development and a former flight attendant. She grew up in Altadena, California in that tumultuous time known as the 1980s. She now resides with her family in the Inland Empire, CA. She's a horror/paranormal romance writer mainly because it feels so good having her characters do bad things and, later,  pondering what makes them so bad and why they can never seem to change their wicked ways.

She enjoys emails from people who like her work. In fact, she loves emails. She can be contacted at tamelamiles@yahoo.com or her Facebook page, Tamela Miles Books. She also welcomes reader reviews and enjoys the feedback from people who love to read as much as she does.

Email: tamelamiles@yahoo.com

facebook.com/sassysleepingbeauties

twitter.com/jackiebrown20

www.ingramcontent.com/pod-product-compliance
Lightning Source LLC
Chambersburg PA
CBHW020145180626
46810CB00004B/1741